TALES
from
PEKING OPERA

by HUANG SHANG

NEW WORLD PRESS
Beijing, China

First Edition   1985

Illustrations: Ma De

ISBN 0-8351-1399-X

Published by
NEW WORLD PRESS
24 Baiwanzhuang Road, Beijing, China

Printed by
FOREIGN LANGUAGES PRINTING HOUSE
19 West Chegongzhuang Road, Beijing, China

Distributed by
CHINA INTERNATIONAL BOOK TRADING CORPORATION
  (Guoji Shudian)
P.O. Box 399, Beijing, China

Printed in the People's Republic of China

CONTENTS

PREFACE

The traditional operas of China as represented by the Peking Opera possess prominent national styles and features. They are an important part of the country's great artistic traditions.

A complex form of stage art that stresses both singing and dancing, the traditional Chinese opera consists primarily of "singing, acting, reciting and fighting", supplemented by dances, typically "round dances", unique costumes and equipment, simple scenery and specially made articles, and accompanied by gongs, drums, strings and bamboos. It is the product of the diligent creative labor of opera workers over the past 1,000 years, during which it has drawn lavishly on both art and life for nourishment. It possesses an extraordinary power of representing life as well as an enchanting artistic appeal, which has enabled it to retain its popularity with the masses down to the present day.

An analogy might be drawn between the traditional opera and the paintings of the great master Qi Baishi (1863-1957), modern exponent of the *xieyi* school that is akin to Western impressionism. Qi Baishi's depictions of grass, flowers and landscapes are in simple, vigorous strokes that leave out many details, yet among the leaves and petals we often see such tiny insects as the dragonfly, cricket and katydid painted in by the *gongbi* (realistic) method with such meticulous care that even the lines on their wings can be seen. The images are vivid and lively irrespective of whether the brushwork is simple or fine, for the two methods are one entity as well as opposites.

In the traditional opera there is an identical or very similar situation. The opera artist may be likened to a connoisseur who has perceived in the vast, colorful and prolific field of life what is primary and indispensable and what is only secondary and may be passed by. The process of formulating according to this principle the whole series of ways and means of presenting traditional operas is almost parallel to the budding, development and prosperity of the "literati's school" in traditional Chinese painting. This is a phenomenon that is not only interesting but worth studying.

"Entrance", "exit", "round dance" and other maneuvers on the traditional opera stage are executed in very simple, economical and clever ways. All restrictions of time and space are removed, giving the actors an extraordinary degree of freedom. Thus such actions as galloping away on horseback, hurrying along a road, threading through a maze of buildings and courtyards, entering a secret room or a lady's chamber, which would be hard to perform in an ordinary play, present very little difficulty here. On the other hand, scenes intended to reveal a character's inmost feelings or to portray acute and violent struggles are never let pass; such scenes must be fully reproduced by all means even if it is like "using the strength of a lion to fight a small hare". The methods of expression in traditional Chinese operas are more varied than in other branches of the performing arts. Facial expressions, the turn of a sleeve, an intricate movement of the body, variations in the singing, modulation of voice, all are means of expressing a character's inner feelings. Bold omissions and minute depictions become a perfectly harmonized entity in the cadence of a carefully worked out plot. The audience enjoys simultaneous audio and visual pleasures, as everything is completed in the same place and at the same time.

The performances of traditional opera artists vary from gross exaggeration to extreme precision. At times the techniques of directing remind us of film making, a relatively modern form of art. It is amazing to audiences how often "close-ups" are used and how well they fit in with the whole performance. The "freedom" enjoyed by traditional opera artists may well be envied by other artists; it is certainly far greater than that enjoyed in any other branch of the performing arts. This "freedom", however, is also self-restricting; it cannot for a moment be divorced from life, nor can it depart from its own "formula".

This "formula" is a product of the creative talent and accumulated wisdom of the traditional opera artists, and assumed its present form only after a long period of sublation and refinement. But as things never cease to grow, the "formula", too, will never cease to change and improve with the passage of time. It is therefore both rigid and flexible in nature.

Classical Chinese operas are mostly based on historical tales, legends and myths, but this does not detract from their artistic charm. The mainstay of their lasting popularity is the vitality of realism. The producer of a classical opera uses the mantle of the ancients, but his handling of the theme and method of presenting the characters are based on the realities of his day. Many of the traditional operas that are being staged today were the "modern dramas" of the era in which they were created and were clearly focused on current realities. For example, the costumes and decorations we are accustomed to seeing on the opera stage today were the vogue of the Ming dynasty (1368-1644), during which operas developed very rapidly and there emerged more "modern dramas" than in any other period of Chinese history.

When first written or produced, classical Chinese operas were always complete stories with complete plots. As the custom of staging performances changed and the interest of audiences gradually focused on one or more aspects of a story, people began to attach greater importance to the most exciting parts than to the whole, that is, they would rather see in one program a medley of compositions from different operas in different styles and ways of presentation. This method of staging operas makes it easier to meet the diversified interests of audiences and to present richer, more refined and more colorful programs.

I was only a child when I first entered a Chinese theater. Very often I merely stood beside the stage and stared with wide-open eyes at what was going on. Since then I have been through many changes, mentally and emotionally, from ignorance to cognition, from less to more, from pure astonishment to sincere admiration, from love of fighting scenes to appreciation of the music and singing. However, first impressions are not easy to erase, and these fragments of opera stories that I have collected in this volume have preserved to a great extent those indelible earliest impressions — impressions that have struck deep at the heartstrings of a child simple but honest, puerile but sincere, able to love and hate without affectation. Because of this, friends who come into contact with this great, exotic and realistic art for the first time may find these writings candid and sincere but not presumptuous.

Huang Shang

Shanghai, 1984

Beauty Defies Tyranny

The Qin dynasty, the first in Chinese history to unite the nation's numerous warring states into one cohesive empire, only lasted for 14 years. The capable but despotic emperor Qin Shi Huang (First Emperor) ruled for 12 years, and was succeeded by one of his sons, the muddleheaded and dissipated Qin Ershi (Second Emperor), who managed to rule for only two years before the empire collapsed. Upon the death of his father, Qin Ershi came to power with the aid of the treacherous minister Zhao Gao, who helped him to topple his elder brother. Once on the throne, the cruel young emperor ordered all of his brothers and sisters slain and interred in a burial pit near his father's tomb. In recent years, archaeological excavations of the tomb of Qin Shi Huang have unearthed not only a small army of life-size terracotta figurines of warriors and horses, but also the skeletal remains of these Qin princes and princesses.

Qin Ershi fell in love with the daughter of Minister Zhao Gao, the comely and intelligent Yanrong, who despised him and therefore had no choice but to feign mental derangement to escape being reduced to the emperor's plaything.

This opera was one in which Mei Lanfang particularly excelled in performing. The role of Yanrong feigning insanity while inwardly seething with hatred for the despotic young emperor, with its compelling mixture of truth and falsehood, is one of the distinctive features of this opera.

— Ed. —

11

Zhao Gao, Prime Minister under the Second Emperor of the Qin dynasty, sat in his study writing an official petition. His daughter, Zhao Yanrong, sat by his side grinding ink for him and arranging his writing paper.

The room was enveloped in silence; on the wall, the dancing shadow of an old plum tree flittered in the moonlight. Father and daughter said nothing to each other. In fact, the only audible sound was the soft monotonous scraping of the inkstick being rubbed on the inkstone.

Dressed in black mourning clothes, Zhao Yanrong was in a state of profound melancholy. Even without makeup, her face glowed with the beauty of a young woman in her prime; with the sadness in her eyes only adding a sense of dignity to her grief. She glanced over at her father, who was totally engrossed in his writing. As her eyes fell upon his long white beard, she was struck with an inexplicable feeling of bewilderment: her father seemed to her like a total stranger; no longer was he the boon companion of a lifetime.

Six months earlier, Zhao Gao had attempted to bribe a minister by offering his son his daughter's hand in marriage. He succeeded in marrying his daughter to this young man, but when the minister refused to cooperate, he lodged false charges against his son-in-law's family and they were all executed. And when his recently widowed daughter returned to live by his side, Zhao Gao, in an extraordinary act of mercy, submitted a petition to the throne requesting a pardon for the family's offences. That these three radically contradictory acts were carried out by a single person left her in a state of extreme perplexity.

It was out of a deep sense of shame that Zhao was drafting that petition to the throne. Considering the influence he wielded at court and the trust placed in him by the young emperor, his petition was sure to be effective. Zhao Yanrong's relief was visible, and for the first time in months she smiled at her father.

Had Zhao Gao had another sudden change of heart? Or had Yanrong regained her father's respect and no longer would be treated as a pawn in his political game of chess? Along with this came a ray of hope, but regardless of whether this was well-founded, it was enough to allow her to believe that she would be able to avoid getting into any further trouble.

Suddenly she noticed a shadow flashing by the window. Before she could identify who it was, she was called back to her room. Her maid, a deafmute, indicated with sign language that the shadow was a man of great prestige and power, and as soon as Zhao Gao saw him, he kneeled down in obeisance. Who would make her father kneel down? And she was told that the shadow had already stood motionless outside the window of the study for quite some time before she knew.

It was not hard to guess who this shadow was. Yanrong's maid told her that while she was away from home during her nuptial proceedings, the shadow had appeared many times at night. Zhao Gao must have prepared a whole variety of delightful entertainments for this mysterious visitor, who never left until well past midnight. Whenever the shadow arrived, Zhao Gao would order everyone away and shut the doors tightly, so the maid knew nothing of what they said or did.

It came as a great surprise when the shadow appeared briefly at the Zhao home and left in hasty this evening. Yanrong was then summoned to her father's presence, and with a big smile on his face he told her how he handed the petition to the emperor in person, and how His Majesty approved its contents at once. Zhao Gao's smile sent an unpleasant chill up his daughter's spine. He was as happy as a hunter who had just bagged a rare prize.

"Congratulations my daughter!" Zhao Gao's joy showed from his eyebrows to the tip of his long white beard. But Zhao Yanrong's face froze, since she knew that no matter how vigorously she protested, it was her fate to remain a pawn, a piece of merchandise, in her father's hands, even though in this "transaction" the "customer's" status was much higher than before. Speaking as if he were delivering an imperial edict at court, he announced, "Tomorrow morning, it's off to the palace with you!"

Yanrong felt she had no friends in the world except for her maid, who had attended Yanrong since she was a child, braving hardships at her side and sharing the deepest secrets of her heart. Though she was incapable of speech, she communicated subtle emotions by means of a set of hand signals which only Yanrong understood. Often it was her maid's cleverness that rescued Yanrong from a whole range of difficult situations.

Though she knew the futility of it, she was determined to protest her father's decision anyway.

"Father, you are a Prime Minister at the imperial court. How could you act with 'a heart so full of shame'?" She began by quoting a phrase from the classical books which she had studied ever since she was a little girl. But her father had no patience to debate this matter with her, and sternly rebuked her. "How dare you disobey your father's instructions? How dare you violate His Majesty's sacred edict?"

These words were the distillation of countless volumes of sagely classical wisdom, and wielded absolute authority in all disputes. In fact, such statements had the power of reducing any appeal to traditional practice or popular morality to a bunch of empty talk.

Yanrong knew she had no way out. As a rational being, she could endure such humiliation no longer. Thus her only choice was to feign madness. With a series of agitated gestures, her maid instructed her to take off her clothing, remove the ornaments from her hair, scratch her face with her nails and roll around on the floor. This was Yanrong's only escape from a lifetime of shame.

Yanrong's strange behavior came as a great shock to her father. After some initial suspicion, he began believing that he had driven her to this unfortunate state. Provocatively, she toyed with the hem of his robe and rubbed up against him. At first she teased him by addressing him as her son and then her husband, and even tried to drag him off to her bedroom. Zhao Gao interpreted her behavior as resulting from the emotional frustrations of a young widow, and her words as an expression of what normal young women kept locked up in the depths of their hearts. He concluded that her behavior was nothing but sheer madness.

For a moment, a pang of paternal remorse passed through Zhao Gao's heart. But this was replaced quickly by a stronger, longer-lasting sense of disappointment inspired by the decline of his daughter's "market value" — from that of a priceless relic to that of a piece of junk.

Unwilling to risk bringing displeasure to the emperor, Zhao Gao escorted his stricken daughter to the emperor's Golden Palace the very next day.

The emperor, who had ascended the throne as a mere boy, was an out and out rogue. Naturally, he had been warned of Yanrong's condition, and this had filled him with suspicion: How could the woman whom he had seen the previous evening with his very own eyes have gone mad overnight? And would his most-trusted Prime Minister dare to deceive him? The emperor placed great trust in Zhao Gao, and believed that he would not dare err in choosing between his own power at court and his daughter's chastity.

Seated on the throne, the emperor watched Yanrong as she stepped out of her sedan chair. Her face bore an expression of profound sadness, and she wore a long cape draped over her shoulders. The scratches she had made on her own face the night before were still visible, but to the young emperor this only added to her beauty. And when she began strutting about with rather undainty strides, he thought she was more beautiful than ever. With a broad smile on her lips, she strutted about the court, waving flirtatiously at the officials in attendance. And as she approached the double row of guards, who with their long-handled weapons held out before them formed a "tunnel of blades", every single soldier stepped back to let her pass.

Since her maid was forbidden to enter the palace, Zhao Yanrong had to face the music alone. This was neither the time nor the place to consider making an escape. In front of her sat the young emperor, surrounded by his many ministers. Her father stood at the emperor's side, whispering into his ear and pointing at Yanrong, like a merchant discussing a shipment of goods.

With every step she took, Yanrong felt her body becoming heavier and heavier. She reminded herself that she had to exercise the greatest caution in order not to expose her deception. Though she had not bowed down to the emperor in the proper fashion, she did address him with a brief "Your Majesty".

Her abnormal behavior was met with a rather conventional response. She laughed out loud at the assembled ministers, but they, following the lead of the emperor, merely smiled back. Suddenly she was struck with the realization that she could not continue in this vein, and began clapping her hands and laughing out loud while running madly about the court room, pointing at the emperor and giggling with the abandon of a little girl.

"You think it's a big joke that I'm insane, don't you? Well, I think it's even more ridiculous that you're nothing but a dissipated old scoundrel!" She continued strolling about in a circle and came up to her father's side. "Older brother, and members of the court: listen to what I have to say. Back when the First Emperor was on the throne, he carried out the sacred sacrifice on Taishan Mountain in the east; he conquered the Five Great Mountains in the south; and he built the Great Wall in the north. He believed that his empire would last for ten thousand years and that country would forever remain at peace. What a far cry he was from you; you unprincipled debauched rogue! This world belongs to all the people; how can a single individual claim it as his won? The way you surround yourself with corrupt officials and indulge yourself in wine, women and song, how long can you expect to remain on the throne?"

At that time and place, only a madman could get away with making such statements. In fact, few madmen ever had such opportunities presented to them. Throughout the entire throne room, not a single sound could be heard. All those present — the great ministers, the emperor's personal servants and the military guards — stood there like wooden dummies, daring not to interrupt or rebuke her. All eyes fell upon Zhao Gao, as if he alone were qualified to judge whether these crazed statements were true or not. Even the emperor seated upon his mighty throne cast a perplexed glance at Zhao Gao, as if to express his regrets for having pressured him into bringing his daughter to the palace. Zhao Gao glared back at the emperor without saying a word.

The entire court room remained absolutely silent.

Yanrong then took off her "phoenix" headdress, removed her tassled cape, rolled them both up together and threw them on the floor. She knew that when feigning madness, there should be no cutting corners, and no limits imposed on her insane prattle. She began stampling on the gown she had thrown on the floor.

"If you continue like this, I'll have your head chopped off!" the young emperor said. He believed that insanity could be cured with a threat of decapitation.

"Yes, yes, yes! Now we'll see if this great emperor truly dares to cut off my head." Yanrong lurched forward, laughing as she spoke. She laughed in such a way that no one there would ever forget it, for she knew quite well that this was possibly her last laugh.

"You know, of course, that once you chop off my head, it'll grow right back again." She had pulled off this entire long performance without a single flaw, but it left her so exhausted that she found it difficult to maintain her self-control. Her final statement was, surprisingly, highly rational, yet not a single person understood what she meant.

Zhao Yanrong finally left the palace. As she dragged herself down the long staircase, she felt as if she would collapse. When she reached the outer gates of the palace, her speechless maid was there to greet her. Falling into her embrace, she broke out crying.

The Pursuit of Han Xin

Before he founded the Han dynasty, Liu Bang once got into a conflict with his enemies during which he relied upon the help of three able men, the so-called "Three Greats" of the early Han dynasty, Xiao He, Zhang Liang and Han Xin.

Liu Bang was initially unaware of Han Xin's ability and entrusted him with only a minor official post, causing him to quit in anger. Hearing that Han had left, Xiao He immediately pursued him and brought him back that very evening.

Later, thanks to Han Xin's brilliance as a military strategist, Liu Bang was able to unite China and found the Han dynasty, which lasted for more than 400 years.

The famed Peking Opera actor Zhou Xinfang first established his reputation by his outstanding portrayal of "Xiao He Pursuing Han Xin by the Light of the Moon".

— Ed. —

The autumn rain pattered on with no signs of letting up. Han Xin, seated in the main hall of the small compound allocated to him as the Director of Provisions in Baocheng, was overwhelmed with a feeling of boredom.

Baocheng was a small city of mud houses with a perimeter of only a few kilometers. Its outer walls were less than three meters high. But now it served as the headquarters of the great King of Hanzhong, Liu Bang. The few decent houses in the city had all been appropriated by the king and his senior officials; what was left to Han Xin, a mere grain officer, was hardly better than a stable. When bored, he would pace the floor of the hall but could not take more than a dozen steps before running into the wall, and this only aggravated his frustration.

In the city it was sand, sand everywhere. There were only two roads and a single intersection. Han Xin, who had neither friends nor relatives nor acquaintances here, harbored an intense dislike for the place. He could hardly believe that it was in this shabby "fortress" that the ancient beauty Bao Si was reputed to have been born; if true, this was indeed a case of "a golden phoenix being born into a chicken's nest". But Liu Bang seemed to be able to tolerate everything about this ghostly place. Day after day he held court, attended to state affairs, put on airs and lost his temper as if life here were normal, full and gratifying. Were there indeed hopes, Han Xin wondered, that this man would do great things someday?

Han Xin had one friend: the little old man, Xiao He, who was Liu Bang's prime minister, was good to him. The day he presented Han Xin to the king, he had consoled him by telling him that the king would use him well. Liu Bang, however, made him the guardian of the grain depot. Standing at the far end of the king's court, Han Xin saw clearly Liu Bang's disinterested look and Xiao He's agitation, which told him more than half the story: Xiao He had recommended him, but Liu Bang had sniffed at the recommendation and a dispute had ensued between the two. He could guess what was Liu Bang's opinion of him.

"Han Xin! That little rascal from Huaiying who asked for alms from a washerwoman and crept between the legs of a scoundrel. If I gave him a high position, would my armies obey me any more? Wouldn't the princes and dukes laugh at me? And what would Xiang Yu say!"

Han Xin was well aware of the stigma he had carried with him all these years. Wherever he went, he had heard nothing different about him. He knew the stigma was wrong and had pinned his hopes on Liu Bang, from whom he expected to hear something different. It was a bitter disappointment.

Xiao He was different from Liu Bang. It seemed that he understood Han Xin's feelings to a certain degree. He was also very polite, possessing none of the overbearing qualities of a prime minister; only his words seemed to carry little weight with the king. Possibly the trouble was that he tended to talk too much; though not really advanced in years, he would, when talking, rattle on endlessly like an old man.

Han Xin saw at once that Liu Bang was a rascal on whom it was useless to waste words. That was why he had not presented Zhang Liang's letter of recommendation, which he had concealed on his person. He was sure that the letter, even though it was from such a prestigious person as Zhang Liang, could have no positive effect on a rascally person.

Now sitting alone in his residence, he reflected on the days when he was a halberd-bearer in Xiang Yu's camp. It was quite clear to him that Xiang Yu was not a rascal, only a good-for-nothing whom he had no need to fear.

But Xiang Yu's man Fan Zeng was an out-and-out rascal and in no way muddleheaded. He knew Han Xin's ability and had suggested to his master that a clever man must be used well or put out of the way; there was no room for hesitation. That was why he had fled Xiang Yu's camp and come to Baocheng. And when he thought this over again, he began to apprehend the dangers of his present position.

He looked about him: there was only a small bedroll and a sword. If he wanted, he could leave at once. On his desk were only a stack of account books, an official seal and an oil lamp. His mind was made up. Picking up the bedroll and buckling on his sword, he went out to the stable, mounted one of the official steeds, and headed for the east gate. As he passed through it, he waved jovially to the officer on guard.

"Off to the countryside to get grain? Have a safe journey!" shouted the officer.

Xiao He was both cautious and kindhearted. He was not a rascal of course, but knew well a rascal's way of thinking and doing things. He was one of Liu Bang's key confidants. When Liu Bang became restless after staying in Baocheng for a time, it was he who counseled him to be patient and to pretend he was content to rule over tiny Hanzhong for the rest of his life. He had also advised the king that if he wanted to seize the whole country someday, it was not enough to rely on his present handful of followers. What he needed was a man of genius like his commander-in-chief.

Taking Xiao He's advice, Liu Bang behaved like a contented King of Hanzhong and at the same time secretly sent out Zhang Liang to find some worthy commander who could help him conquer Chu (Xiang

Yu's kingdom) and establish the Han dynasty. This man was to come to him with Zhang Liang's letter of recommendation. Unfortunately, a difference rose between Liu Bang and Xiao He in their estimate of Han Xin's ability.

Xiao He found himself beset with difficulties on both sides. On the one hand, he had done everything he could to persuade the king to give Han Xin an important post, but had only succeeded in having him promoted by one grade. It was most disappointing and there seemed to be no hope of promoting him over the heads of the king's other officers. On the other hand, he had to convince Han Xin of the need to be patient; he had to speak out for his master, trying to make Han Xin believe that the king, after all, was a sensible person.

Both tasks were difficult. Han Xin was a clever man and it was no use flattering him; on several occasions he had shown his displeasure at Xiao He's long-windedness. The prime minister was indeed in a tough spot.

On this day Xiao He was up before dawn. He stood in the courtyard with his eyes half-closed looking upwards. The sky was full of stars, for the rain that had continued for days had finally ended. This livened up his spirits somewhat and as he rubbed his hands briskly, he kept muttering something under his breath. There was no one nearby. He was merely talking to himself, repeating over and over: "I've got to go and see Han Xin." Though it was below the dignity of a prime minister to call on a grain officer, Xiao He had done this a number of times.

He called out to the gatekeeper to harness his carriage, but there was no response. Assuming that it was because the gatehouse was too far away and his orders had not been heard, he called again. In a short while, the keeper came limping up with a frightened look on his face: "General Han has fled!"

"Who told you?"

"The officer guarding the east gate saw him leave for the country to collect grain. That was two days ago and he hasn't returned yet."

On hearing this, Xiao He set aside the dignity of a prime minister as well as his own years. Usually a careful man, he did not care to ask much this time; the news must be true, for he had long anticipated it, though not as soon as this. He paced the courtyard in quick steps, enquired briefly about Han Xin's clothes and whether he had taken his personal belongings, and then gave orders to saddle his horse.

"Can Your Excellency ride a horse? You always travel by carriage," asked the keeper skeptically.

"Fool! Hurry up and ready my horse!" Xiao He had lost control of himself.

The keeper led two horses over, followed by a sturdy bodyguard. Xiao He in his long robes and high boots was helped into the saddle with some difficulty. He had a hard time finding the stirrups and the keeper had to squeeze his boots into them. As he sat shakily in the saddle, a gust of wind nearly blew his hat off. He pressed it down and the brim covered his eyebrows. With his eyes fixed straight ahead, he gave his steed a tap with the whip and it sped like an arrow out of the front gate.

The streets were full of mud, which the flying hooves of the horses splashed in all directions, forcing passers-by to take shelter under the nearest eaves. From there they watched the two riders, especially Xiao He, a specter sitting bolt upright like a door plank.

The thoughts that turned in Xiao He's mind as he rode along were much the same as those of Fan Zeng, for there was one principle that both men believed in. Talented people should be won over to one's own side, the more the better; but if that could not be done, the next best thing was to dismiss them because it would be disastrous if they went over to the enemy. He and Fan Zeng had served in rival camps that had fought each other hundreds of times, and it was through long, hard experience that they arrived at this truth. But Xiao He was more optimistic: he was sure he could get Han Xin back, so there was no need to plan his death; the man could still be put to great use. His reasoning was based on an understanding that Liu Bang and Xiang Yu were radically different persons.

After passing through the east gate, they saw before them a series of low hills with a single narrow path winding through them. Notwithstanding the rain, which had ceased only a short while ago, the marks of horse hooves could be seen clearly. Xiao He gave his horse a few hard kicks and it bolted forward. At a sharp turning in the road, the furious beast threw off its rider and trotted away to nibble at the green grass at the roadside. When the guard rode up, he found the prime minister leaning against a large tree, his brocade robes already half soaked with muddy water.

The guard helped him into the saddle again and they rode on for another half day. It was high noon now and both men and horses were exhausted, hungry and thirsty. Not far in front they spotted a cliff, at the foot of which was a thick growth of greenery with a small cascade that hung there like a pearled curtain. There must be a deep pool beneath it, which was just what they needed. The neighing of a horse now broke the silence. They hurried on a few more steps and there, sitting beside the pool, his horse tied to an old tree nearby, was the object of their pursuit.

The three stood there motionless, eyeing each other for some time. Seeing the prime minister's sorry appearance, Han Xin could not help laughing. There was no need for words; everything was clear.

"What's the hurry! I was just going to call on you when they told me you had run away. How could you! Everything'll be all right; I've spoken to the king again...." Xiao He rattled on, but Han Xin only listened with a smile.

"I'll take out Zhang Liang's letter when I see Liu Bang," Han Xin thought to himself. "Looks like he won't take me at my word without a letter of recommendation."

The three horses trotted leisurely back over the small muddy path, which by then had dried up.

A Foolish Dream

This opera deals with how Zhu Maichen's wife, Madame Cui, looked down upon him for being poor and divorced him to marry another. Afterwards, when Zhu Maichen attained rank and power, Madame Cui was filled with regret. One evening she had a dream in which she envisioned that she was still married to her former husband and that someone had been dispatched to present her with a phoenix coronet and a silk cape, the costume of a high official's wife. But in the midst of her delight she imagined that her present husband suddenly appeared with an ax. Awaking in fear, she gazed all around her and felt terribly grieved to see the dilapidated walls of her present surroundings.

Zhu Maichen (?-115 B.C.), a real historical figure, was an official during the reign of Emperor Wu Di during the Han dynasty, but his actual deeds were of little historical importance. However, since almost every genre of Chinese traditional opera features works based on the theme of Zhu Maichen rejecting his former wife, his name is well known throughout China.

This is a traditional item in the repertoire of Kunqu Opera, a genre which originated during the Yuan dynasty in Jiangsu Province. By the late 16th century it gradually began to spread to other areas and exert a considerable influence on Sichuan and Peking Operas. Furthermore, each of these genres of traditional Chinese opera contain items with arias set to Kunqu tunes. The melodies of Kunqu Opera are especially subtle, their movements are graceful and their lyrics are elegant. During the late Qing dynasty, this form of opera entered a period of decline. However, after the establishment of new China, with state support, Kunqu Opera was revived and a new generation of talented performers emerged, of whom perhaps the most representative is Zhang Jiqing in the role of Madame Cui.

— Ed. —

Of late, Madame Cui would always go to the front door and stand there for a while after her midday meal. Very often she would fall into a state of both complacency and uneasiness that was hard to explain, and sometimes she even seemed to be in a trance. It all resulted from a sudden change in her life. Formerly a wife who constantly had to worry about her next meal, she was now sufficiently well off to enjoy simple homely fare all the time, and the change had relieved her of so much housework that she did not know what to be done with her hands and feet, as if they were not content to be idle. So she would pass the time at the front door, gazing at the green Lanke Hills in the distance and the winding footpath beneath them; and as she did so, visions of the past rose like dreams, or nightmares, that could not be dispelled.

Quite often she would stare blankly at the foot of the hills for almost half a day, musing on her past, recalling how she had limped down the hill along that narrow path. No, it wasn't easy! Just before her first marriage, her parents had exhorted her to remember the popular saying: "A good horse will not take a second saddle; a

31

good girl will not marry a second time." Remembering this, she had time and again suppressed "inappropriate" ideas and remained faithful through many difficult years to that pedant Zhu Maichen who knew nothing besides reading books. It was this idiotic pedant who, when forced to cut firewood for a living, would place a book upon his load and recite as he walked along, and not infrequently from being too engrossed, would trip and fall by the roadside. It both amused and vexed her when she recalled these absurdities, but now, at last, she had escaped from that hopeless family. And she heaved a long sigh.

She still remembered that in the beginning she had believed him when he told her that palaces of gold, royal four-horse coaches, phoenix coronets, rosy capes, trains of maidservants... all would come through reading books. Zhu was a kind and good-tempered husband. As she lay in his arms and listened to his beautiful tales of the future, she not only believed it all but was quite enchanted. Even now, she saw him, not as a braggart, but as an honest man. If he was to be blamed, it was only because he himself, like one possessed, also believed the stories and was not trying to deceive his beloved but miserable wife. In time, however, she "realized" that they were mere fantasies, dreams that would never come true. Of course, the gossip of the women in the neighborhood also had some affect on her. "Such a young girl, and as pretty as a flower. How long will you go on living with that half-crazy bookworm? Don't be taken in by all that nonsense. When will noble horses and sedans ever come to this poor valley?"

When she reflected on all this now, Madame Cui's heart would soften with a slight compunction. The pedant

32

was not a likable person, to be sure, but he was different from her present husband. What she had gained from the change was security from cold and hunger, but what was it that she had lost? She could not say even though she had been weighing all the time the consequences of the decisive step she had taken. It was a piece of reckoning that could not be made clear.

Though she did not regret the step, she could not help harboring a slight feeling of guilt, especially over the events of the last night when she finally hardened her heart and forced her husband into signing the divorce paper. She shuddered whenever she thought of it. Was she really such a mean person? It was all planned out with the help of that woman who lived next door: "This is your only way out; otherwise you'll just have to stick to him and die together of hunger or cold!"

That fateful night, gritting her teeth, she decided to resort to this last measure. The poor husband was stupefied. When she thrust a brush into his hand and bade him sign the paper, his hand shook like that of a child ordered by a stern teacher to trace the characters in a copybook. She forced him to sign his name, stroke by stroke, and then snatched the paper away and thrust it in her bosom. Zhu collapsed like a heap of clay, speechless and expressionless. The only sound in the room at the time was the sneering laughter of the woman as she turned and walked away.

When she recalled that scene now, a cold shiver ran down her back. She vowed many times never to think of it again, yet always in her pensive moods it was the first to reappear in her mind.

She turned her dreamy eyes from the foot of the distant hills to the main road and hailed some of her new neighbors who were passing by. These women all smiled at her to be sure, but somehow she sensed a bit of malice behind those smiles. A silly notion! She decided to go back into the house.

As she pushed open the door, two men dressed like public servants called to her from behind in a voice that was unusually courteous. They addressed her as "Aunt" and were asking the way to the newly appointed Prefect of Kuaiji to offer their congratulations. It sounded a little strange. The Prefect of Kuaiji was a high-ranking official governing several counties. Why did these people come all the way to this small valley to look for him instead of going to some large town?

"Where does His Lordship Zhu live?" they asked.

Madame Cui's heart skipped a beat: "What Lordship Zhu?"

"Zhu Maichen, His Lordship Zhu."

"He?" Madame Cui felt a sudden dizziness and wondered if she was not dreaming. As her manner suggested that she knew something, the men greeted her again and asked, "Lady, you know where he lives?"

She turned and pointed towards the Lanke Hills, but could only nod her head continually, seeming to have lost her voice. Finally, after some effort, she stammered out, "His Lordship Zhu.... He ... he lives at the foot of those hills", and with these words she sent them away.

Alone in the house, she took out the bowls of rice and vegetables from the kitchen cupboard and sat down to supper. After sitting there a while, she put them away again, forgetting that she had not yet taken a mouthful. Next she lit the lamp, rolled out the bedding and sat down beside the bed but did not undress. She did feel very tired and wanted to sleep, but it was still too early. And it wouldn't do just to sit there doing nothing. The crickets in the corner began singing and this only added to her annoyance.

Her eyes moved with the flicker of the oil lamp. She was listening attentively. The sounds in the streets gradually died down. One after another her neighbors closed and bolted their doors. Soon there were no more human sounds or voices anywhere, only the singing of the crickets in the wall.

Could it all be true? Did those men find that pedant? If they didn't, they should come back and ask again; but if they did, she would hear from them no more. How she regretted that she had not asked the two men in for a cup of tea and told them that the prefect's wife lived right here. . . . Why not? After all, she had left Zhu Maichen's house only a short time ago and, as far as she knew, he had not remarried.

The singing of the crickets sounded a little strange tonight. Maybe she had not noticed it before since she had heard it too often, but now as she listened carefully, there seemed to be both rhyme and rhythm to the singing. All of a sudden a large piece of snuff formed in the wick of the lamp; it charred and the sparks it gave off turned into a bright flash. . . .

Who was that knocking so impatiently at the door? Had the two officials come back? Madame Cui jumped out of bed and hurried over to open the door. Yes, it was those two officials, but they were not alone. Behind them was a train of *yamen* servants, including a woman, and seven or eight runners each holding a large tray of red lacquer. As she stood there not knowing what to do, the servants all knelt down reverently, which shocked her so much that she, too, dropped on her knees. But the woman-servant immediately helped her to her feet and escorted her to a chair. The runners now knelt down one by one and held the red lacquer trays above their heads.

"We are here on the orders of His Lordship to escort Your Lady to your post."

Madame Cui calmed herself as she looked down upon the kneeling party. She held her body stiffly without moving a muscle; for in her mind now the most important thing was not to lose the dignity of a prefect's wife and bring disgrace on His Lordship. Just then when the servants were paying their respects, it was a terrible thing for her to fall on her knees too. But then, what exactly were the proprieties of a prefect's wife? She had no idea. Instinctively, she began blaming that pedant for not coming here to fetch her himself.

"His Lordship Zhu...."

"His Lordship, on the orders of the Emperor, has hurried away to assume his new post. Before he left, he sent your humble servants here to escort Your Lady to his place," interrupted the head servant. The woman-servant now stood up, took over the red tray from one of the runners and walked up to her.

"Lady, here is the phoenix coronet and rosy cape!" she said as if these were the tokens of their mission. Her eyes were dazzled by the brilliance — the glittering pearls set in a crown of gold, silver and jade. In the past she had only seen such things on the stage while sitting far away in the stall. Occasionally, Zhu Maichen had described to her the shape and make-up of a coronet; but unfortunately she had always interrupted him. She felt some compunction when she thought about it now. He was a loving, warm-hearted husband after all to have sent her this coronet.

    As she sat there like one in a trance, the head servant
made a gesture, at which the runners took out musical
instruments and began playing on them. It frightened her
a bit at first. The woman-servant who was standing by
picked up the coronet and placed it squarely upon her
head, then with great courtesy helped her to her feet and
wrapped the cape round her shoulders. It was a piece of
bright red brocade with a pattern of the sea and pheasants
embroidered in gold. Supported by the woman, she took a
few unsteady steps, feeling somewhat dizzy. She was
moving to the music of drums and flutes, and as she did so

she looked down in front and saw only an expanse of red whose brilliance nearly blinded her. She blinked and slowly let out a smile of pleasure and satisfaction. Never, she thought, since she was married into the Zhu family, had she smiled so contentedly — it was a smile from the bottom of her heart, a smile with reverberations deep within.

Now she really needed some sleep. She had felt totally exhausted before it happened, and now after all this excitement she lost control of herself and collapsed upon the table. A very long time seemed to have passed. Seated in the official sedan-chair, she was carried a long, long way before she finally reached the prefect's residence. Amid an explosion of fireworks, the two heavy black lacquered gates swung open with a loud squeak and there was Zhu Maichen, in his red official robes, smiling at her as he walked out of the main hall. She was all nervous and in a hurry to step out of the sedan. In doing so, however, she knocked her head against the lintel above the door....

Another large piece of snuff flared up in the wick of the lamp and the room gradually darkened. Madame Cui was seized with terror. Everything was gone — the *yamen* servants and runners, the sedan carriers, the phoenix coronet, the rosy cape... even the smiling Zhu Maichen in his red robes.

The music was gone, too. There was only the singing of the crickets, which sounded louder and harsher than ever. A half-moon rose above the broken garden wall, its beams illuminating the room with a silvery light.

The Capture and Release of Cao Cao

Towards the end of the Eastern Han dynasty (25-220 A.D.), power at court fell into the hands of a wicked official, Dong Zhuo. When his attempt on Dong Zhuo's life failed, the young Cao Cao fled, and was arrested as he passed through Zhongmou County by Chen Gong, the county magistrate.

Out of sympathy for Cao Cao's actions, Chen Gong set Cao Cao free, and decided to join him on his flight.

In traditional Chinese drama and fiction, Cao Cao is portrayed as the epitome of undisguised treachery.

— Ed. —

As Cao Cao galloped down the road, a rabbit suddenly darted across the horse's path and plunged into the wild grass at the roadside. Cao Cao reigned his horse to a halt, cursed the "little demon", and stopped for a rest.

On this winter evening in northern Henan Province, the grassy yellow-earth plains stretched nearly treeless as far as the eye could see. Far off in the distance was a sparse copse, with the setting sun hanging above the trees, white and bloodless like the face of an invalid. Looking around him, Cao Cao could see no sign of life and sighed. He then turned to watch the approach of Chen Gong, who was whipping his horse with all his might, yet still unable to speed the animal along. Chen appeared as a small blue dot on the horizon, wriggling back and forth, gradually becoming larger as he approached. Cao Cao sighed again: fleeing with this kind of bookworm in tow was such an encumbrance. Cao Cao frowned, his long slanting eyebrows coming together in the center of his forehead. His dusty face was pale save for two patches of color dotting his cheekbones, but his eyes still held their old sparkle: quick and penetrating, they flashed with determination and vigilance.

Cao Cao mused: When I regain command of my own troops and have more of a free hand to get things done, Chen Gong will be an outstanding adviser, fully worthy of being my aide-de-camp. Since he's such a poor rider, he can be given a sedan chair. . . . But what about now? Two fugitive generals fleeing alone, like two men with three legs. . . .

Cao Cao felt the deepest respect and gratitude for Chen Gong. Cao Cao had been captured in Zhongmou County, but with a few words had convinced Chen Gong, the Zhongmou County magistrate, not only to release him, but also to accompany him in flight. Where on earth could one find such a good man, such a righteous man, such a fool! He pushed aside a strong desire to flee on his own, but felt ashamed of himself and spat noisily onto the ground.

Chen Gong finally managed to catch up. Gasping with his mouth open and his hands tightly clutching the reins, he gazed up wide-eyed at Cao Cao. Side by side they rode westwards.

"There's probably a manor house beyond that copse ahead," Chen Gong said. After leaving Zhongmou County the night before, they had traveled a full day without resting. Chen Gong was on his last legs, but didn't dare propose stopping for a rest, and just gazed at Cao Cao.

"True enough, we need a rest. The horses are exhausted, too. But we don't know if the people who live in the village are friends or enemies." Chen Gong made no reply. They continued on as before, their horses constantly stretching their necks to graze at either side of the road in an attempt to assuage their hunger.

A figure suddenly came into view on a side road and Cao Cao straightened up in the saddle. Seeing it was only an old villager, he relaxed and sat down again. The old man stopped, and shouted at them in a loud voice:

"Mengde.* Isn't that Mengde on the horse?"

Cao Cao was so startled that the color drained from his face. He urged Chen Gong forward.

"Lü is my family name. Your father stayed in my home last night, but left hurriedly this morning. He never imagined that you would come."

Chen Gong thought that running into any old acquaintances at this stage could only bode evil. But he could not convince Cao Cao, and they followed the old man into the manor.

Cao Cao and Chen Gong sat facing each other in the manor hall.

Their host was very hospitable. He sat them down and ordered his servants to prepare food and wine, and personally took a blue and white patterned wine jug to the next village to buy wine. A cautious Chen Gong quietly interrogated Cao Cao about the old man's background.

---

*Mengde is one of Cao Cao's other names.

Cao Cao smiled: "Don't worry. Lü Boshe was my father's sworn brother and our two families have been close for years. Being here is the same as being at home." Then he sighed, "It's just that my father has fled from home, and goodness knows where he has gone for shelter!"

The two men fell silent. They were both thinking of Lü Boshe, an aged man, walking slowly to the next village which must be four or five *li* away. Cao Cao raised his head and looked at the darkening sky. A young servant, smiling broadly, carried a lamp into the room and set it down on the table. Still smiling, he gazed at Cao Cao until Cao Cao became irritated by the smile. Cao Cao stretched out a hand to touch the wide-brimmed blue hat he wore. The fish-tail creases at the corner of his eyes seemed deeper than ever.

From the kitchen someone called the young servant's name and he immediately turned and ran off, two long, coarse hemp ropes tied around his waist swinging behind him. Cao Cao watched him silently.

After a day and a half of steady travel, what they wanted most was to unroll their bedding and sleep, but this was impossible; they could only sit there and do nothing.

Cao Cao, longing to doze off, strolled over to the window for a look at the view of the courtyards. The tiny courtyard contained a flower bed, and next to it he could see a huge kitchen connecting to the back courtyard. From the back courtyard he could hear the sound of pigs feeding — or was this an outhouse? He gazed for a long time and then returned to his seat.

Suddenly his drowsiness left him. He pricked up his ears and looked at Chen Gong.

"Listen! What's that?"

"It sounds like a knife being sharpened."

Chen Gong was right. But why? This one question could have many explanations. The thought triggered off a whole string of questions in Cao Cao's mind like the sparks emitted by the fuse of a fire cracker. Cao Cao instinctively stroked the knife he had unbuckled from his waist and placed on the table. Why had the servant boy smiled at me like that? Why was that rope hanging from his waist? Why didn't the old man send him to buy the wine, but insist on going himself? It was not possible that the boy could not manage to fetch a jug of wine. Some things can't be explained to a child; but a simple thing like fetching wine?

Cao Cao felt his hair stand on end, and his nostrils quivered.

"What are you going to do?" Chen Gong said, when he noticed Cao Cao unsheathe his knife.

"I'm going to take a look around!"

Chen Gong, unable to utter a sound, watched with his eyes wide open as Cao Cao quietly slipped out of the door like a puff of wind.

A short while later Cao Cao returned, eyes reddened, but laughing to himself.

"I've killed them, killed all of them, every single member of their family. I slew everyone one by one from the kitchen to the backyard to the main hall. Only when I reached the pigsty did I see they had used the rope to truss the pig to the rafters. . . ." Cao Cao beamed, and barely seemed aware of Chen Gong's presence.

Chen Gong was struck dumb. He had only met Cao Cao two days before, but he had immediately been impressed by his haughty, straightforward manner and bold speech. This was a heroic youth with uncommon

43

ambitions, courage and resourcefulness. These qualities had convinced him to place his life in Cao Cao's hands, abandon his post and accompany him in flight. He had not known that Cao Cao was a man who would commit innumerable errors than change his ways.

To Chen Gong, Cao Cao had suddenly become a different man. In Zhongmou County, Cao Cao had addressed him as "Your Honor", and on the road had treated him as a friend. But now he was ordering him about like a servant. Cao Cao became even calmer, and ignoring Chen Gong's protests, firmly ordered him to clean up the place, lead the horses from the stables, take kindling straw from the kitchen and spread it in the courtyard, and then find some live cinders. . . .

As they mounted their horses and left the manor, the fire was burning fiercely, thanks to a strong north wind which had whipped it to a brilliant blaze in minutes. At the first intersection, they encountered the ill-fated Lü Boshe returning from the next village. Before he knew it, he had fallen at the roadside with a stroke from Cao Cao's blade.

"It's best to let him go with the rest," Cao Cao told his speechless, wide-eyed companion. "If he went back home, he'd go crazy; he'd report to the village constable, the filthy dog!" Cao Cao cleared his throat. "I still have many things to do. I can't let a soft heart get in the way of important affairs. If I'm wrong, I'll be wrong right to the finish! We'll settle the final account later. Understand?" Cao Cao finished speaking and whippecd his horse's rump, urging it forward.

They arrived at an inn.

Cao Cao told the innkeeper to give the horses plenty of fodder, then ordered five jugs of wine, two plates of meat, and tucked into a large meal. Chen Gong watched silently from the side. Cao Cao didn't speak. He knew what Chen Gong had to say, and felt no need to reply — he'd already explained everything to him earlier on. After finishing his meat and downing half the wine, Cao Cao unbuckled his knife, stripped off his coat, rolled it into a pillow, and lay down on it and fell asleep.

At dawn the next morning, he awoke to the sound of sparrows twittering noisily under the eaves outside his window. Opening his eyes, he gazed around the room. Everything was gone. Jerking himself into a standing position, Cao Cao leapt off the bed and saw a letter on the table weighted down with his own knife.

Cao Cao opened the letter and read slowly, a malicious smile spreading across his face. "Useless fool!" he bellowed. The sound of his voice was so loud that he even terrified himself.

The Long Slope

This opera recounts the story of the conflict which took place between Liu Bei and Cao Cao during the late Eastern Han dynasty, when China was split into three warring factions. These factions later developed into three antagonistic countries which existed in a state of tripartite confrontation for approximately half a century (220-280 A.D.). Various versions of the story occur in the repertoire of Peking Opera, other forms of Chinese traditional opera as well as the genres of "jingyun dagu" (storytelling in the Beijing dialect with drum accompaniment) and "kuaishu" (rhythmic storytelling to the accompaniment of copper clappers). The protagonists in this opera are the valiant general Zhao Yun and the wife of Liu Bei. The libretto of this opera was substantially revised by Yang Xiaolou, a famed "wusheng", and Wang Yaoqing, who played the role of "dan" in command performances before the Qing court. It is their revised version which is still being performed today.

— *Ed.* —

Followed by a large retinue, Cao Cao galloped up the slope of a small hill he had chosen as a lookout. He rode leisurely around its peak, examining the terrain on every side: beneath him was a mulberry forest and further on an open plain; to the east was a small river, beyond which rose another hill. He was satisfied that he had

47

chosen a well-sheltered spot, for an observer looking upwards from below could only see the mulberries, while from the top all movements on the battlefield were visible.

There was a slight smile on Cao Cao's face. As he was not a man who habitually smiled, this was a rare moment for him; though he did his best to conceal his feelings, the smile nevertheless appeared. He had good reason to be pleased, for since the battle began everything seemed to have proceeded according to plan. Liu Bei's small force was sure to be wiped out. His only worry now was that Liu Bei might flee too fast and escape to some faraway place where he could hide and remain a potential threat. But quite surprisingly Liu Bei's withdrawal was very slow; according to reports from the field, his movements had been hampered by a flood of refugees. It puzzled Cao Cao that he had not run off by himself.

With such an ideal battleground before him, Cao Cao intended to throw in all his forces here to destroy the enemy completely. All his generals had been sent into battle, even Xiahou En, the custodian of his prized Green Rainbow Sword. Only Cao Hong, his cousin, remained behind to act as a messenger to transmit his orders and report occasionally on the progress of the battle. The others were nonmilitary personnel, his advisers and counselors, among whom was one who had remained silent throughout — Xu Shu.

Cao Cao was a man who valued talent. In the course of many years of political and military struggle, he had firmly grasped the truth that men of ability were important if not indispensable to the success of his cause. And his experience told him that he needed good counselors no less than good fighters, and that different tactics must be used in dealing with different people. Today he had purposely kept Xu Shu at his side and conversed with him kindly, for he wanted him to witness with his own eyes Liu Bei's disastrous defeat and annihilation. This silent but exceedingly clever man, up to now a close friend of Liu Bei's, might be persuaded by the grim realities to change his allegiance. . . .

"Mr. Yuanzhi (Xu Shu's courtesy title), this is indeed a good battlefield. If everything goes well, the battle will be over before nightfall," remarked Cao Cao, scanning the foot of the hill and talking to himself. The corner of Xu Shu's mouth seemed to twitch slightly, but no sound came. Perhaps his reply had been smothered by a sudden roll of drums.

Cao Cao pricked up his ears at the sound of the drums and the shouts that followed. They seemed to come from around a curve in the hill. Strange to say, there was none of the din and whoop of two armies clashing. The sounds all seemed to come from his own troops and were approaching steadily like a tide. The next minute a solitary white figure on a white horse rounded the curve, brandishing a sword that continually emitted flashes of silvery light.

Cao Cao recognized this as an enemy general and nodded slightly. It must be that he was being lured to this open place to be ambushed and killed. Sure enough, following the white horse were two of his own generals, Xu Chu and Zhang He, in black battle dress and on black steeds. They were pursuing the white horse closely.

At the edge of the river the white knight suddenly reined in and turned his horse around. Surprised by this move, Zhang He also checked his horse. The two eyed each other for a few seconds, then a flash of white light rose and Zhang He raised his lance to ward off the blow.

In an instant, the white horse had sped past him and disappeared again around the curve.

Up on the hill Cao Cao snorted in disgust. Things did not go according to his plans just then. How was it that an enemy general could come and go so freely among his troops? And why were both Xu Chu and Zhang He panic-stricken and powerless to stop him? Cao Cao turned his head slightly and at this bidding Cao Hong edged up to him.

"Go and see what this is all about," he commanded.

Xu Shu had recognized the white knight, but he was also perplexed as to why he had appeared so suddenly among Cao Cao's troops and just as suddenly disappeared again.

"That was Zhao Zilong (Zhao Yun) of Changshan, Zhao the Fourth General," he said, "a tiger of a warrior."

Not even the people in Liu Bei's camp, let alone Cao Cao and Xu Shu, could guess the reason for Zhao Yun's taking this seemingly motiveless risk that was more like a child's game. Liu Bei's followers had been scattered and each was fleeing on his own. His two wives and infant son, Ah Dou, were lost too. Only Zhao Yun was at his side and this faithful general now took upon himself the task of finding and escorting back the two ladies and Liu Bei's heir. So instead of following the retreat he had turned around and charged into the ranks of the enemy. Even the formidable Zhang Fei (Liu Bei's sworn brother) was astounded at this: Zhao Yun must be mad, or perhaps he was giving himself up to Cao Cao.

Zhao Yun's actions seemed mad. Alone and armed with a single lance, he had fought his way into the thick of Cao Cao's army that numbered close to 100,000 men. When he rounded the curve, he saw before him an open

plain on which there were no signs of stragglers or fleeing troops; and since he was in no mood to fight Zhang He and the others, he turned around and galloped off in another direction.

Zhang He was brought before Cao Cao to make a report. He could offer no plausible reason for Zhao Yun's

conduct and only cursed, "That damned fellow! Let me lure him to this place again and we'll have the archers hidden among the mulberry shoot at him until he looks like a hedgehog." As he spoke, he cast a glance sideways at Xu Shu, who was standing beside Cao Cao.

Cao Cao's face was a blank; he said nothing. But Zhang He's steed kept rapping its front hooves as if in agitation. Xu Shu now spoke, but whispered as if he did not want to be heard: "This is indeed a great warrior; there's not one like him in a thousand!"

Meanwhile, the white knight on the white horse had reappeared around the curve. This time it was because he wanted to break through Cao Cao's encirclement and the open plain seemed a likely place. He had completed more than half his mission, for he had unexpectedly come upon Lady Mi, one of Liu Bei's two wives, sitting badly wounded beside the wall of a village house. She had handed him the infant Ah Dou and he had carefully placed the baby inside his breast plate next to his chest. As he did this, Lady Mi turned and leaped into a dry well. Though shocked and grieved, Zhao Yun was consoled by the fact that the most important part of his mission had been completed in spite of all the dangers and hardships. He knew, by feudal standards, what a woman and her only son were worth. For a woman, the most important thing was to preserve her chastity, especially in the present chaotic conditions of war. Now that the lady had found her peace at the bottom of a well, there was nothing more to worry about. But the infant Ah Dou was another case. This baby was the scion of the imperial Liu family, the legitimate heir to the throne of Han.... His life was of inestimable value.

In the eyes of Cao Cao and his followers on the hill, Zhao Yun was a different man now, more daring, more powerful and more reckless than ever before. Cold steel besieged him on all sides; clashes of iron resounded in the distance; but neither man nor metal could stop him. The

54

white knight was literally fighting his way over a path of blood.

The frost on Cao Cao's face melted. He alone recognized the weapon in Zhao Yun's hand: it was his own Green Rainbow Sword, a weapon that could "slash through iron like clay". And he knew well how it came into Zhao Yun's possession. The sword was precious, but more precious was the man who now wielded it. The best sword in the world was useless in the hands of a good-for-nothing who could not even defend his own head. An inordinate and irrepressible desire to win over this gallant white knight burned fiercely in Cao Cao's breast. He looked around at his followers, at Zhang He, and at his soldiers and generals who in trying to stop Zhao Yun were being cut down one after the other. Turning to Cao Hong, he issued his orders:

"Zhao Yun must not be sniped at. He must be captured alive. Anyone disobeying these orders shall be executed."

Meanwhile, Zhao Yun found it strange that while he had fought so hard and so well, he had not been struck by a single arrow. Zhang He too wondered why the Prime Minister should be willing to pay such a high price for the capture of Zhao Yun. He did not know that Cao Cao had no interest in a "hedgehog".

When the Prime Minister's orders were announced, his troops began closing in upon the lone white knight from all sides, but none dared let fly an arrow. Even those who engaged him in combat had to be careful about their blows. If only he could be thrown off his horse, seized and bound! But that did not happen, and Zhao Yun pressed ahead.

Zhao Yun fought bravely until he had driven them to the side of a brook. From afar he saw Zhang Fei's black banners through the trees and the dust storm created by the tree branches tied to the tails of the horses ridden by Zhang Fei's men. Zhao Yun slipped away from the soldiers swarming about him and charged down a trail which led away from the main road. He then turned back abruptly and from a bridgehead saw Zhang Fei riding his horse with his long spear in hand.

Before long, Zhao Yun came upon Liu Bei and his party in the depths of another forest about a mile from the bridgehead. Dejected, they were resting on the ground. Zhao Yun was glad to see his master and quickly dismounted from his horse. Liu Bei asked him:

"You returned all by yourself?"

Suddenly Zhao Yun remembered that Ah Dou was concealed in his breast. Zhao Yun turned around and carefully removed his armor and inner garments. Ah Dou was peacefully asleep there, his plump little face snuggled up in Zhao Yun's sweating breast.

With Ah Dou cradled in his arms, Zhao Yun quickly turned around, and without a word presented the child to Liu Bei. Liu Bei was stunned and for a long while didn't know what to say.

The Dragon and the Phoenix Show Their Colors

In the late Han dynasty, after a large-scale peasant uprising, political power in China gradually became divided between three factions headed by Cao Cao, Liu Bei, and Sun Quan respectively. After Cao Cao's death, these three factions became the basis of the Three Kingdoms, which governed China for half a century.

The highly influential ancient Chinese novel "The Romance of the Three Kingdoms" chronicles how the factions headed by Liu Bei and Sun Quan united against that of Cao Cao in a power struggle. This novel depicts Liu Bei as being both the true descendant of the royal family as well as a model statesman.

This frequently performed Peking Opera is known under the various titles "The Dragon and the Phoenix Show Their Colors", "Ganlu (Sweet Dew) Temple" and "Liu Bei Gets Married". Among its most outstanding features is the lengthy aria in which Qiao Xuan urges the Empress Dowager of the Kingdom of Wu to take Liu Bei as her son-in-law. One of the reasons why this opera's popularity has remained undiminished for so many years is that it includes the full range of Chinese operatic roles: "sheng", "dan", "jing", and "chou".

— Ed. —

Liu Bei sat perturbed on a boat floating down the Changjiang (Yangtze) River; paying no attention to the fine scenery along the way. He was upset about the famous statesman and strategist Zhuge Liang. He had made three visits to Zhuge Liang's thatched hut finally succeeding in persuading this "Sleeping Dragon" to give up his temporary retirement from the political arena. Ever since, Liu Bei had relied on Zhuge Liang's strategies and schemes, and as a result Liu Bei's troops survived numerous difficulties, and grew in strength. Zhuge Liang had proven himself to be a trustworthy person of extraordinary ability as a strategist. His faults were that he often decided things on his own in an arbitrary way, and seemed reluctant to confer with Liu Bei. For instance, Liu Bei's traveling down the river to marry into the Sun family of the Kingdom of Wu was all arranged by Zhuge Liang. Although Liu Bei was not entirely willing to enter into this marriage, the boat was already heading for Wu. Liu Bei had not the slightest idea of whether his adventure would turn out to be a success or a disaster. When he saw Liu Bei off, Zhuge Liang had smiled and said, "Take it easy. I'll take care of the rest." But what did he have up his sleeve? Liu Bei no longer felt he was the emperor's uncle, but simply a card in Zhuge Liang's hand.... He was becoming more upset each moment.

Liu Bei felt a greater sense of security when he realized that his brother-in-arms, Zhao Yun, was standing beside him, dressed in full armor. Zhao Yun was a brave and loyal general who could hold his own in a battle of ten thousand. But this time they were going to an enemy state. Who could guarantee that Zhao Yun could bring him out alive if the going got rough?

Liu Bei recalled that before leaving home, Zhuge Liang had conferred privately with ZhaoYun; but it was rash for him to make any inquires at this point, so he feigned calm, and said casually, "Brother Zhao, this trip to the Kingdom of Wu to marry into the Sun family is a rather uncommon one, so we must be more careful."

"Don't worry, master. Zhuge Liang has given me an embroidered pouch containing three ingenious plots."

From Zhao Yun's expression, Liu Bei could sense the prestige Zhuge Liang enjoyed among the generals and soldiers. When Zhao Yun gave him the embroidered pouch, he began to feel that maybe it was unnecessary to have any suspicion about this military counselor.

From the embroidered purse he removed a piece of paper on which many abstruse poems were written. Liu Bei frowned when he realized these poems resembled the inscriptions used by fortune tellers. As he read on, he discovered two sentences which seemed more palpable than the rest: "When the two of you arrive at the Kingdom of Wu, you should call on Qiao Xuan." Liu Bei's frown turned into a smile.

Qiao Xuan was actually a key figure who could provide solutions to critical problems. The two men who held the actual power in the Kingdom of Wu were Sun Quan and Zhou Yu, who along with their generals, commanders and soldiers, seemed to be hostile and indignant towards Liu Bei's occupation of Jingzhou. Qiao Xuan was the only person in power who was not committed in this fashion.

Zhao Yun knew little about Qiao Xuan, so Liu Bei introduced him briefly:

"Qiao Xuan has two daughters, both famous beauties. The older Qiao had married Sun Quan's older brother, Sun Ce, who was dead, and the younger was Zhou Yu's wife. Actually, Qiao Xuan is the father-in-law of the Kingdom of Wu! After we arrive and get settled, prepare some generous gifts and we'll call Qiao Xuan."

A civil officer, Lü Fan, and a military officer, Jia Hua, were sent to receive Liu Bei. Both were close associates of Sun Quan. They felt relieved now. The turtle was on the hook at last.

Qiao Xuan was the military chief and the governor of the Kingdom of Wu. He was held in high esteem by the members of the older generation and had intimate relationships with the founders of the kingdom, Sun Jian and Sun Ce. Also through marriage, he had gained influence with Sun Quan's mother — Wu Guotai.

But in the eyes of Sun Quan and Zhou Yu, Qiao Xuan was nothing more than a decrepit and fatuous old man, a stumbling block on their road to advancement. For instance, using marriage as a plot to take Liu Bei as a hostage in exchange for the return of the territory of Jingzhou was an idea developed by Sun Quan and Zhou Yu, Qiao Xuan knew nothing about it. In terms of military strategy, Qiao Xuan and Lu Su could be considered conservatives. They advocated uniting with Liu Bei to fight Cao Cao, the sovereign of the Kingdom of Wei. Sun Quan and Zhou Yu were rather displeased with this strategy. Qiao Xuan was a hindrance to their political goals. Yet because of his prestige, they could not do anything about him at this point.

On the way back from court, Qiao Xuan noticed that the street was decorated with lanterns and colored streamers and that the local people had extraordinary cheerful expressions on their faces. There was also something unusual taking place at his own house: the members of his family were going around whispering things to each other. When he questioned his old servant Qiao Fu and learned he was the only one still in the dark, he became angry. But at that very moment, it was announced that Liu Bei had arrived.

The visit was formal and brief. Liu Bei presented a generous gift to the Qiao family. After seeing Liu Bei off, Qiao Xuan decided to go to the palace to visit with the King's mother, Wu Guotai, and sound her out. That he had not been informed of such an unusual political marriage made him both furious and suspicious that something tricky was involved. From his point of view, the marriage of the Sun and Liu families was in fact a good thing, for it would align previously hostile forces against Cao Cao, though there was a possibility that Sun Quan and Zhou Yu would fail to give their approval. There was something fishy about the whole business!

Qiao Xuan was surprised to discover that he was not alone in his ignorance of the marriage. When he learned that even Sun Quan's mother, Wu Guotai, did not know about it, Qiao Xuan said to her, "Since even Your Ladyship knew nothing about this great affair, who could have made the arrangement?"

"That's right, who's idea was it?"

"Perhaps we should consult our sovereign...."

Qiao Xuan's suggestion was entirely reasonable and seemed to embody no personal feelings. Sun Quan was then summoned to the court.

Sun Quan was a tall, well-built man with ruddy cheeks and a beautiful bushy moustache which inspired people to call him "Purple Beard" behind his back. He carried on his father and brother's career and gathered around himself a group of young generals. He was a local ruler of lofty aspirations and great ideals. Nevertheless, he was both respectful of and submissive to his mother. He understood that the people who stood behind his mother were a bunch of old-timers like Qiao Xuan, whom had to be dealt with delicately.

Sun Quan sat down next to his mother and felt a twinge of disappointment when he discovered that Qiao Xuan was already there. Wu Guotai asked him directly: "Is the marriage between the Sun and Liu families your idea?" Sun Quan became flustered and glanced hostilely at Qiao Xuan. When he replied "Well, I ... I don't have any idea," Wu Guotai pulled a long face to evince her displeasure. Sun Quan now realized he could hide the facts no longer and made a clean breast of the whole story.

Wu Guotai's criticism of Sun Quan and Zhou Yu's plan was hard to refute. She put it this way: "Since Liu Bei refuses to return the long-occupied territory of Jingzhou, you should have deployed troops to fight him, and seize it back by force. But you've chosen to use your own sister as bait; so even if you gain back Jingzhou, won't you be making a fool of yourself in front of everybody?"

Qiao Xuan stood up and added a few words of his own. And in order to silence Qiao Xuan, Sun Quan pointed out that it was Qiao Xuan's own son-in-law who was the chief plotter.

"Zhou Yu again! He obviously wants to get you in trouble!"

"Shut up!" Sun Quan could speak rudely to Qiao Xuan, but he had little choice but pretend obedience to his mother. In any case, the plot to kill Liu Bei had been hatched secretly, and he would make no compromise on that score.

Wu Guotai was furious about her beloved daughter

being used as a bait in a scheme of entrapment. This was a violation of the dignity of the Sun family. As for murdering Liu Bei, this was a matter to which she gave little attention. With this in mind, Qiao Xuan made sure to leave her with a favorable impression of Liu Bei and of his extensive authority in the State of Shu.

In the eyes of Sun Quan, Qiao Xuan was nothing more than a clown. But in front of Wu Guotai, he assumed the role of a storyteller and recounted Liu Bei's glorious family background and dazzling military accomplishments. He told her how Liu Bei's ancestors were members of the Han dynasty imperial family, and listed the heroic exploits of his famous brothers-in-arms: Guan Yu, with his Blue Dragon Sword; Zhang Fei, with his long spear; Zhao Yun with his military triumphs which took place at the Long Slope; and the brilliant strategist Zhuge Liang. Of course, Sun Quan hated listening to all that, but Wu Guotai was completely charmed. No matter how many times Sun Quan winked at Qiao Xuan to stop, the old fellow went on talking with great zest, ending up with a strong recommendation that the marriage knot should be tied.

Sun Quan flared up at last: "In any case, Liu Bei isn't good enough for my sister!"

"He certainly is!" Qiao Xuan wouldn't give an inch either.

Wu Guotai put an end to the quarrel by deciding to meet Liu Bei the next day at the Temple of Sweet Dew.

"What if you do find him acceptable?" Qiao Xuan asked.

"Then he'll become my son-in-law."

"What if mother doesn't like him?" Sun Quan asked immediately.

63

"Then you'll take care of him. You may go now!"

Sun Quan felt confident about the outcome and left with satisfaction. Since Liu Bei's fate would be decided the next day, Qiao Xuan could not help worrying about the criteria she would use in making her decision.

In the less than two days' time, remaining many decisions had to be made concerning the fate of Liu Bei and the Kingdom of Wu.

"Liu Bei's hair is already graying: he hardly resembles a young groom, I can hardly imagine my honorable mother finding him acceptable." The more Sun Quan thought about it, the more upset he became. What a nuisance it was that Qiao Xuan had hands in this business. Who could predict what sort of malicious remarks he would make. At present, a number of generals had set separatist regimes of their own, although the Han Emperor was but a single card in Cao Cao's hand: If you poked through the ashes, there was a good chance of finding some burning embers. Cao Cao's prestige had spread throughout the whole nation, particularly in east. In terms of class origin and family status, the Sun family could not match the Liu family. Therefore, it was very likely that Wu Guotai would find it advantageous to have a rich son-in-law. All this made Sun Quan sharpen his vigilance.

Sun Quan summoned Lü Fan to the court to discuss counter measures. They decided to organize a group of assassins to ambush Liu Bei in the Temple of Sweet Dew, and assigned General Jia Hua to be the commander. They were determined to kill Liu Bei no matter what took place at the meeting between Wu Guotai and Liu Bei.

What worried Qiao Xuan most of all was not Liu Bei's class origin but his gray beard, which might not pass his future mother-in-law's inspection.

When Qiao Xuan arrived at his home, he sent a messenger to deliver some black hair coloring to Liu Bei and instruct him how to use it, so that he would appear at least ten years younger than his present age. In addition, Liu Bei was warned of a possible ruse being carried out at his expense during the meeting, and was advised to have his generals wear armors inside their military robes in the event a fight should break out.

The great hall of the Temple of Sweet Dew was all arranged for a banquet, with bright red table cloths and chair covers. Naturally, the center seat was reserved for Wu Guotai, and the seat of honor beside her for her future "son-in-law". Ceremonial guards and court officials were all busy decorating the hall, setting out wine and fruit, and arranging the tables and chairs. At the same time, generals and soldiers wearing civilian dress were also busy secreting swords and knives in strategic places in the corridors and wings of the temple. Jia Hua flitted about observing the activities taking place in the front hall; he was fully armored and well-equipped with whips, cudgels and swords; with his hand he constantly fiddled with a large knife.

At this moment, Wu Guotai arrived, accompanied by Qiao Xuan, and was led to her seat of honor. Liu Bei arrived shortly afterwards. Exquisite music echoed through the palace hall. Following Wu Guotai's orders, Qiao Xuan stepped forward to greet Liu Bei. He clasped Liu Bei's hands tightly and examined his dyed beard. Qiao Xuan was pleased and whispered to Liu Bei, "That's Wu Guotai seated there. You ought to bow to her!"

Liu Bei nodded knowingly.

"You are the present Emperor's uncle. How can I

possibly accept such a great honor?" Perhaps in response to this polite formula, Wu Guotai remained seated there with extreme calmness. Then, Qiao Xuan broke the silence, "Your Royal Highness, it's only proper for our new groom to pay his respects to you." He then turned to Liu Bei and said: "It's only polite for you to offer several additional bows to her."

Liu Bei knew how to satisfy the King Mother's sense of self-esteem; he also understood the significance of his bows and the effect they would have. Therefore, he bowed in the most solemn and respectful fashion, which pleased the seated Wu Guotai to no end. Next, Zhao Yun was ushered into the hall. Wu Guotai was extremely pleased with all that had gone on so far. But at the same time, she was annoyed that Sun Quan and Zhou Yu had arranged things in such a fashion. When she noticed that Sun Quan had not come, she said, "Call Sun Quan!"

When he arrived, he paid his respects to his mother and only unwillingly greeted Liu Bei. His eyes never left Qiao Xuan, who flatteringly escorted Liu Bei to his seat and then sat down on his right hand side. Sun Quan was so disgusted that he felt like he had swallowed soap.

The conversation now turned to the subject of the new groom's family background. Liu Bei spoke of his family tree and his experiences in a calm and unpretentious manner. Occasionally, Qiao Xuan would chime in with some additional details, to which the King Mother listened with great pleasure. But, all this only enraged Sun Quan further.

Qiao Xuan next praised Liu Bei's facial features, "He has phoenix's eyes with the eyebrows of a dragon; his ears hang down to his shoulders; his hands extend below his knees." This, to Sun Quan, meant that he was nothing

66

more than a "Big-Eared Crook". The brave military accomplishments and lofty aspirations of Guan Yu, Zhang Fei and Zhao Yun were lauded to the skies by Qiao Xuan. Sun Quan naturally found this recitation unbearable and first warned Qiao Xuan to talk less and conserve his energy. But, when Qiao Xuan went on to relate how Zhuge Liang "borrowed the east wind to burn down the whole army of Cao Cao under the Red Cliff", Sun Quan could bear it no longer and let out with a mighty roar.

"Zhuge Liang's fire seems to have fried your brain, so everything you say is nonsense!"

Lü Fan entered and requested Sun Quan to issue an official document. An official document? The truth was that Lü Fan had waited too long and was impatient for Sun Quan to lead the attack.

Sun Quan donned an arrow-proof tunic and girded on his long sword. With the fully armored General Jia Hua and a small group of trained killers behind him Sun Quan set out from the back corridor and was met by additional soldiers and horses, forming a line which resembled a long snake.

Itching for battle, they watched Sun Quan starting to pluck his treasured sword from its scabbard. They were all ready to make an all-out attack, when Sun Quan suddenly hesitated.

"Jia Hua!"

"Yes!" Jia Hua held a long saber tightly in his hand.

"Withdraw the troops for a length of an arrow shot!" Sun Quan's voice quivered with excitement.

"Hey!" Jia Hua sighed deeply, assembled troops and withdrew into the long corridor.

At the same time, Wu Guotai's meeting with her future son-in-law ended triumphantly. Qiao Xuan was appointed to preside over the wedding ceremony, and an auspicious day and hour had to be selected. The "Emperor's uncle" was about to become the "beloved son-in-law".

At the King Mother's banquet, Zhao Yun could hardly keep his mind on the food and drink. He heard the clicking of weapons, the twittering of voices, saw the movements of the killers in the distance. Zhao Yun approached Liu Bei and whispered to him that soldiers

and weapons had surrounded the Temple of Sweet Dew. Liu Bei turned around and kneeled down in front of Wu Guotai.

Wu Guotai became extremely angry, and inquired about who was acting in such an unprincipled manner. Qiao Xuan said, "I'm afraid this was our Royal Highness' idea." Thus Sun Quan and Lü Fan were summoned to the hall of the temple, though they denied any knowledge of the affair. But Jia Hua's denial came to nought, and Wu Guotai ordered to have him decapitated. Liu Bei stood up and pleaded for him, "Killing this person on such a day as today is unpropitious!"

While walking towards the bedroom of his bride Sun Shangxiang, Liu Bei could not rid himself of the sense of danger which had been plaguing him. Ever since he arrived in the Kingdom of Wu, it seemed that traps were set to ensnare him at each step he took. He kept Zhao Yun at his side at all times, even during the wedding party.

The mission entrusted to Zhao Yun by Zhuge Liang was to protect Liu Bei. But the rules were rigid, and Zhao was not allowed free access to the palace.

Liu Bei was greeted at the palace gate by rows of knives, their icy radiance glimmering in the red lamplight like rows of icicles. He thought to himself, "Is it any way to a decorated bridal chamber?" Zhao Yun left and Liu Bei was completely alone.

While the court ladies opened the palace gate, they beheld their new master standing in a trance.

The sumptuously dressed bride, Sun Shangxiang, was seated in her bridal chamber holding a lantern. She smiled when she was informed that her husband refused to come in before the armored palace guards withdrew.

"He's spent most of his life in the battlefield; now he's afraid of this?" She ordered the armored guards to withdraw.

Sun Shangxiang readily accepted the marriage her mother had arranged for her. But it wasn't until the wedding night that she learned she was being used as political bait. From her husband's hesitant manner, she could guess there was more to this marriage than met the eye. Shangxiang was smart; though she didn't participate in state affairs, she greatly concerned about the safety and well-being of the Kingdom of Wu, and for this reason, she was well disposed towards Liu Bei from the very beginning. But why was he so afraid of ordinary weapons? And why did he talk about the dangerous situation he was in and ask for protection? "I have been a wanderer most of my life; and never had a home to call my own. It is my greatest fortune to marry you today, but the one thing that worries me is that your brother Sun Quan is trying to kill me...."

Sun Shangxiang could only rely on Wu Guotai to offer them protection. But, the political situation changed every minute—something beyond the control of their marriage relationship. They could live very happily together, but they both knew that this happiness was not necessarily permanent.

Zhou Yu, the leading admiral of the Kingdom of Wu, had displayed his extraordinary skills in the battle of the Red Cliff wherein Cao Cao was defeated. Thus, he and Sun Quan spearheaded the recovery of Jingzhou. Their plot of entrapment had met with objections and was rebuked by Wu Guotai and the senior statesmen and high officials. Therefore, changing their plans became inevitable. From Zhou Yu's point of view, the once make-

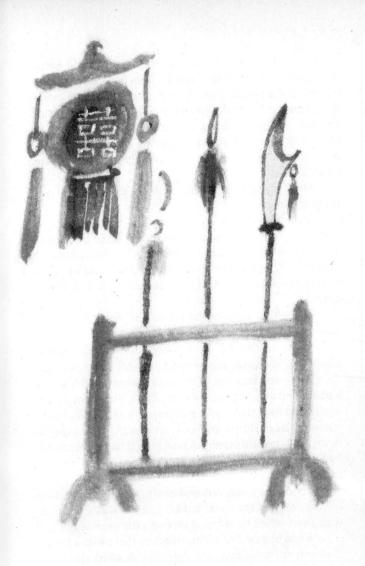

believe marriage had become a reality, so they'd better make the best of a bad thing. The new plan was to embellish the palace with all sorts of luxuries, and assign more court ladies to dance and sing so that Liu Bei would become indulgent. This would gradually sap his will and make him forget all about Jingzhou. This sinister design would be easy to carry out and unlikely to meet with any objections.

Their joyful married life went on as peacefully as a running stream.

Zhao Yun was lonely living by himself on the post. It had been a long time since he had last seen Liu Bei, and he never ceased thinking about the responsibilities entrusted to him by Zhuge Liang: to protect Liu Bei, and to return to Jingzhou by the end of the year. Now, it was almost time.

Zhao Yun decided to go to the court to see his master.

When he entered the heavily guarded rear palace, Zhao Yun heard the faint sound of flutes and drums and the singing and laughter of the court ladies. He felt as if he had entered a strange new world. Zhao Yun waited alone in the entrance hall, feeling cramped and uneasy in this strange place. He paced back and forth, stretching his limbs, and suddenly realized how long it had been since he had last sat astride a war-horse, or executed military exercises.

Giving the appearance of having been dragged away from a feast by the court ladies, Liu Bei was still flirting with them when he stepped through the gate of the hall.

When he saw Zhao Yun standing there with a look of discomfort on his face, Liu Bei was shocked and said,

"Brother, why are you still here?"

"Without your orders, where can I go?" Zhao Yun replied.

"Back to Jingzhou!"

"I cannot leave you alone here."

"But you must go," Liu Bei said with a smile. "Tell our other brothers and Zhuge Liang not to worry about me."

"If you don't go back, who will handle the military and state affairs?"

"Let Zhuge Liang take over. You must be bored all alone in the guest house. There are so many beautiful court ladies and delightful maidens here, why don't you pick a few out to accompany you!"

Impatiently, Liu Bei turned around in readiness to leave. Zhao Yun had never been snobbed in this manner before. He remembered that Liu Bei occasionally got angry and lost his temper, but it was never as severe as this. Now, he was acting as if he were another person, as if he had completely cut himself off from the past.

Zhao Yun wondered how he could rescue Liu Bei from this abnormal situation. But he knew there was nothing he could do.

The awkward silence between them was suddenly broken by a stirring tune played by the court musicians. This music seemed to make Zhao Yun realize that only Zhuge Liang could save Liu Bei from further dissipation. Although Zhuge Liang the man was far away, his wise counsel was hidden in the embroidered purse.

Zhao Yun turned around, gently loosened his armor, removed the pouch, and carefully read the second strategy. Smiling broadly Zhao Yun walked to Liu Bei and whispered in his ear: "Zhuge Liang sent me a message

75

saying that Cao Cao is seeking revenge for his defeat at the Red Cliff. He is now leading an army in the direction of Jingzhou."

Sun Shangxiang learned that Zhao Yun had come to see her husband and became suspicious when he failed to return. Zhao Yun had been away from the court for a

long time, and if something important hadn't happened, he would not have come at all.

Their warm, happy married life had gradually cured Liu Bei's anxiety. He seldom mentioned the generals who were still camped at Jingzhou, nor did he worry about the threat from the younger faction within the Kingdom of Wu. Though Sun Shangxiang took great pleasure in her married life, she was constantly feeling pains of conscience over the fact that Liu Bei had sacrificed his entire military career for her sake. Was there any reason for her to be proud about this? Shangxiang was no ordinary woman; she had always been charmed by military life. Her happy marriage to Liu Bei made her realize that her own life was inextricably tied up with his career.

It appeared that at the time Liu Bei had no contact with Jingzhou; in this respect, Zhao Yun would be the only hope. Now that Zhao Yun had returned, and it appeared like this connection was coming back to life.

Sun Shangxiang slowed her pace so that she would be able to overhear Liu Bei and Zhao Yun's conversation. They were discussing how to return to Jingzhou, and whether or not they should tell Sun Shangxiang about it. Zhao Yun believed that once Sun Shangxiang found out, they would never get away. Liu Bei cried out, "My princess, I must flee!" Liu Bei's words sent Sun Shangxiang's heart, and she could hardly move. She observed Liu Bei in the front hall; he looked absent-minded and panic-stricken, and was speaking incoherently. After repeated inquiries, he told her that Cao Cao was attacking Jingzhou. Although Sun Shangxiang knew nothing of Zhuge Liang's wise counsel, she was clear-minded enough to realize that what Liu Bei said was only an excuse. But what surprised Liu Bei the most was

Sun Shangxiang's immediate decision. She said: "Since you are so concerned about the fate of your kingdom, I will accompany you after I report to mother."

Liu Bei threw himself at Sun Shangxiang's feet and began to sob.

When Sun Shangxiang went ot take leave of her mother, she could not intimate that this might be her final farewell, but said instead that she was going to accompany Liu Bei to the river bank to sweep their ancestors' graves. However, seeing her daughter's face covered with tears, Wu Guotai pressed Sun Shangxiang for the truth. After learning the real reason for their journey, Wu Guotai gave her daughter her approval, and they parted in tears. Just as Sun Shangxiang was walking out, her mother called to her: "You will have to pass by the Violet Mulberry Pass on this trip, perhaps Zhou Yu will not let you out!"

Wu Guotai presented her daughter with an imperial sword and said, "If anyone tries to block your way, you may kill him. I will personally bear the responsibility." Sun Shangxiang kneeled down before Wu Guotai, knowing that she was still her mother's beloved daughter. But she wondered: was she still the sister of the man who handled the military and state of the Kingdom of Wu?

Zhou Yu was an astute man. He had been a military commander since the age of 34, and in the battle of the Red Cliff, both laid a foundation for the Kingdom of Wu and established a high reputation for himself. He and Lu Su were both in favor of war, and were instrumental in arranging the cooperation between Sun and Liu in the battle of the Red Cliff. Zhou Yu was a young man with a vigorous spirit and a reluctance to admit defeat: he always acted according to his own will. The failure of the

entrapment plot annoyed him no end. Since he had
married the younger daughter of Qiao Xuan, he became a
relative of the Suns; from then on everything had
proceeded smoothly, and all his military strategies were
carried out with success. Only this time, when things went
against his wishes, he could not help but feel that he had
lost face.

Zhou Yu could see his enemies multiplying before his very eyes. The man who had seized Jingzhou had become the "son-in-law" of the Kingdom of Wu; and then there was cold-hearted Zhuge Liang, whose smiles couldn't conceal his malicious intentions. The worse thing of all was that his partner, Lu Su, who had always concurred with him, had recently come up with differing opinions. So now he was confronted not only with external enemies, but by antagonistic currents within the ranks. He had already put much effort into talking Lu Su over to his side, but he remained as immovable as a tree. Under these circumstances, Zhou Yu's feelings of helplessness intensified to the point where they were becoming hard to control.

In order to conceal his weak position, revive his personal prestige, and resolve internal contradictions, Zhou Yu announced that he was carrying out a new strategy: Liu Bei would be imprisoned in the Kingdom of Wu for the rest of life; his military forces would be dispersed, enabling the Kingdom of Wu to gradually dissolve the strength of the Kingdom of Shu and achieve the goal of recovering Jingzhou. Suspended between doubt and belief, Sun Quan was finally persuaded to follow Zhou Yu; but Lu Su had never given in. However, Zhou Yu was smart enough to realize that keeping Liu Bei in captivity was a bad plan in the long run, particularly since he had already become a "son-in-law" to the Kingdom of Wu.

Zhou Yu carried out his duties in a leisurely fashion yet with dignity of a great general. His headquarters were located Violet Mulberry, a place of strategic importance near to Liu Bei's forces. Missions of inspection and reconnaissance become more frequent; and all who passed by the headquarters were subject to interrogation, in order to prevent spies from crossing the border. Zhou Yu was quite satisfied with these arrangements, he still felt uneasy.

Bad news was sure to come at last: Liu Bei and his wife were on their way to Jingzhou. Zhou Yu jumped when he heard the news; while the soldiers began to assemble, Lu Su stepped into Zhou Yu's tent and said, "There is nothing wrong with Liu Bei, bringing his wife back to Jingzhou. Why are you sending soldiers after them?"

"It was difficult enough getting him to leave Wu. How can we just let him go so easily!" Zhou Yu replied.

"I'm afraid the King Mother would disagree with you," said Lu Su.

"Sun Quan would certainly back me!"

"What if troops are being sent out from Jingzhou?"

"I would be in charge of the defense!"

"Zhuge Liang isn't easily provoked!" Lu Su said without hesitation.

This was a familiar argument for both of them. Lu Su had never dared to stir up unpleasant memories in Zhou Yu, though he did mention the name of the one person Zhou Yu detested the most. Lu Su could do nothing to stop Zhou Yu, and a group of soldiers and horses set off after Liu Bei and his party.

Ding Feng and Xu Sheng were the two generals leading the troops. They first saw Liu Bei's carts and horses hastening forward in the distance, though because they had not rested since setting out, the pace of the group seemed to be slowing. Liu Bei, on horseback, led the group, followed by Sun Shangxiang's cart. Zhao Yun brought up the rear. They had most likely noticed the soldiers, and realizing how difficult it would be to break away from them, finally halted on the slope.

Ding Feng also ordered a halt, but was hesitant about making an instant attack.

Zhao Yun knew this was the right time to read Zhuge Liang's final message of wise counsel. The message was to have Sun Shangxiang rescue them from the siege, since the fight at that point would have been unwise.

Sun Shangxiang dismounted from her cart. Brushing aside the hair on her forehead with her hand, she stood there calmly, viewing the distant troops as if she were enjoying a beautiful natural scene. Zhao Yun, standing by her side, was holding the imperial sword given to her by Wu Guotai. Liu Bei hid himself behind them in a place from where he could see everything that was going on.

Ding Feng and his troops led their horses forward and stopped at the foot of the slope. They paid homage to Sun Shangxiang, but did not fail to notice Liu Bei.

"Ding Feng, Xu Sheng, Jiang Qin, Zhou Tai!" one by one, Sun Shangxiang majestically called out the four generals' names. "What are you here for?"

"We are here with orders from Sun Quan. Your Highness and your honorable husband are requested to return." These were the words Zhou Yu had entrusted them with before they left.

"Though you are under orders, we are making this trip back to Jingzhou with the blessings of the King Mother." She turned around and winked at Zhao Yun. "Zhao Yun, show them the imperial sword presented to us by the King Mother. Whoever dare to block our way will be killed."

Ding Feng and his followers could only stand there and watch helplessly as Liu Bei mounted his horse and rode off. Zhao Yun was the last to mount, and rode off with a sneer on his face, wielding the imperial sword, as if saying good-by to a group of friends seeing him off.

On the way back, Ding Feng's group met with Zhou Yu's which came up from behind. And shortly afterwards, Zhou Yu's soldiers caught up with Liu Bei's party. For a second time, it fell upon Sun Shangxiang to step forward and speak, and what followed was a mere repetition of what had gone on before. Zhou Yu failed to present any better reasons to justify his actions, and only ended up battling one-to-one with Zhao Yun. Though there were no casualties, Liu Bei's group made up while their swords were still clashing.

Even a high official like Zhou Yu was rendered powerless by that imperial sword. Pursuing Liu Bei seemed to be the only way to deal with the situation, and Zhou Yu put his last hopes on the nearby Changjiang River.

A small rowboat emerged from the nearly endless patch of reeds growing in the river. The man standing on the bow, Zhang Fei, was dressed like a fisherman in black clothing, and had on straw sandals and a round straw hat edged with black. His eyes glistened, and his dark face was flushed with excitement. He had been waiting there for a long time, gazing over the vast expanse of river. Finally he noticed curls of flying dust in the distance. He knew this signaled the arrival of horses and carts, but it was too early to judge whether these were the important guests he was expecting.

Liu Bei's party finally arrived at the big river, where all of Zhou Yu's hopes lay.

Standing on the bank, Liu Bei turned around and saw Zhou Yu's troops approaching and felt that the end was near.

Zhao Yun first noticed a few black shadows in the reed bushes. As they grew larger, it became clear that they were a group of small bark boats. Finally Zhao Yun could see that it was Zhuge Liang, holding white feather fan in his hand.

This was a most unexpected surprise, particularly for Zhang Fei. He fondled his long beard, which hung down to his chest, and bounced about like a child, greeting and chatting with those who had just arrived. He was also greatly concerned with his brother-in-arms Liu Bei. How many times had he appealed to Zhuge Liang before the master strategist finally promised him the job of receiving Liu Bei. Zhang Fei led 3,000 soldiers and horses disguised as fishermen, and took cover in the reeds. Impatience led him to lose confidence in Zhuge Liang, but finally when everything turned out just as Zhuge Liang predicted, he made a special visit to praise Zhuge Liang's brilliant foresight. Zhang Fei spoke highly of Zhao Yun's efforts in escorting Liu Bei back safely. Later, Liu Bei took Zhang Fei to meet his bride, and he shyly kneeled down to pay his respect. Sun Shangxiang smiled at him winsomely and said, "There's no need to be so polite!" Her grace and beauty came as a pleasant surprise to Zhang Fei, who had never met such a person before. Her sweet-sounding voice was intoxicating to him, and he turned to someone beside him, made a funny face, and tried to imitate her voice; but nobody understood what he was mumbling about.

Zhuge Liang arranged for Liu Bei and Sun Shangxiang to get a boat, and handed the task to Zhang Fei. In a twinkling, the river became quiet again.

A war broke out at the foot of the slope not far from the river. What confronted Zhou Yu at this time was not the imperial sword of Wu Guotai, but Zhang Fei's long serpent spear. He knew though that he would fail miserably. In the meantime, at a higher point on the slope, there was a group of soldiers dressed in black assembled in rows, who were jumping about and shouting with delight:

> *Zhou Yu thought he had a plan,*
> *To take the whole world in his hands.*
> *He failed to snare with feminine charms,*
> *And finally lost in the contest of arms.*

This was a perfect reflection of Zhuge Liang's strategy, and made a neat conclusion for the little battle.

The Ruse of the Empty City

During the latter period of the Three Kingdoms (220-265 A.D.) the Kingdom of Wei, which was ruled by Cao Cao's descendants, was increasing in power while the Kingdom of Shu, governed by Zhuge Liang, was getting progressively weaker. Just at this time, the commander-in-chief of the Wei army, Sima Yi, marshaled his troops to attack a city in Shu located near the border between the two kingdoms. Completely taken off guard by this surprise attack, Zhuge Liang, the minister of Shu, had no time to prepare an adequate defense of the city. Famous for his resourcefulness in military strategy, Zhuge Liang landed upon the stratagem of deceiving the Wei troops into retreating by making them believe that the besieged city was defended by a large army. This incident, which is recounted in the novel "The Romance of the Three Kingdoms", is well known to all Chinese people.

In China, if someone has prophetic powers or is extremely resourceful, he is often referred to as being a "Zhuge Liang".

— Ed. —

Zhuge Liang was a little weary. These last few years the military expeditions against the north had become a heavy burden on the Kingdom of Shu — and weighed particularly heavily on him personally. He had recently begun to feel that he was engaged in an impossible job, yet he knew that he must keep working at. These last few years he had to make an extra effort to brace himself in order to get things done. To the people and soldiers, scholars and officials of Shu, their Prime Minister appeared to be full of vim and vigor; but he himself was well aware that he had lost much of his energy, and that his appetite was worsening daily. When he returned to his inner room from the hall, he would slump down into his chair, unwilling — and nearly unable — to move.

But still his mind could not relax. The planning of this latest campaign — from formulation to implementation — had seriously taxed his energies. He had sent General Zhao Yun to attack Baocheng in order to divert the attention of the Wei army, and would then personally lead the main forces towards Qishan Mountain.

Appointed by the Kingdom of Wei to lead its resistance force was the veteran general Zhang He. Zhuge Liang pondered deeply before deciding to send Ma Su as commander of a forward division to garrison Jieting. Ma Su was an experienced advisor, who had always participated in the planning of military strategy for the late emperor. A deeply learned man, he had put forward many valuable ideas. In addition, he had cooperated with Zhuge Liang for years and was familiar with his military strategies. His only shortcoming was a lack of practical experience. Sending him out to take command of the operation was a last resort, which would at least ensure that no naive moves would be made. This notion made Zhuge Liang more at ease, so he diverted his attention by looking around him. But there was no one in sight. His two young attendants understood the Prime Minister's temperament, and knew that he liked to rest alone in his inner room. Was he actually resting; it was difficult to say. His attendants dared neither to enter the room nor to wander too far. They were ready at all times for his summons. Sometimes they would peep through a crack in the door and see the Prime Minister pacing up and down the room, holding the feather fan which never left his hand. Sometimes he would intently gaze at it as if examining an intricate design on its surface. Once one of his young attendants secretly looked at the fan, but all he could see was a beautiful arrangement of black and white goose feathers.

Now Zhuge Liang was once more pacing the room with the fan in his hand, but he wasn't looking at it. Occasionally he would pause and stare up at the ceiling, although it was quite empty save for a huge old spider web suspended between the rafters, with a large spider resting peacefully in its center.

What was Zhuge Liang thinking about? He was recalling the smile on Ma Su's face as he received his orders. Perhaps Ma was a little excited at being given the responsibility of commanding a contingent of infantry and cavalry for the first time but on the other hand perhaps not. Zhuge Liang couldn't suppress a rising suspicion, but quickly consoled himself. Before setting out, Zhuge Liang had discussed in great detail the terrain of the area and its surface features, as well as the method of striking camp and the battle order to be adopted, explaining these things to the bearded general as if he were a small child. This was one of Zhuge Liang's peculiarities. But although Ma Su agreed readily to everything he proposed, it could be seen from his face that he had not absorbed what was being said. But Ma had already left, and in the past he had always obeyed his directions, so there should be nothing to worry about.

Zhuge Liang remained in his room for a long time. He ate and drank but felt no desire to rest. Unaccountably his spirits had soared and he was not in the least sleepy. He watched the sun set.

In his mind's eye, Zhuge Liang followed Ma Su setting out at the head of his army, completing the long journey and arriving at Jieting. According to his own instructions, guards would be posted, the local terrain would be surveyed and camp pitched. They would then begin on a map of the area which would be sent back to Zhuge Liang by fast horse. At the latest it should arrive in another quarter of an hour. The main camp remained peaceful and quiet, both inside and out. There was not a sound to be heard.

A complacent smile touched Zhuge Liang's face. This was discipline born of his own long-term administration of the army. Even if his own camp had contained hundreds of thousands of soldiers, it would still be just as quiet as this. But he quickly recalled that all his soldiers had been led away by Zhao Yun and Ma Su, and that this time the silence was real. All he could hear was the occasional muffled coughing of a few old soldiers, the sound clear and lonely in the night air.

It was only after the oil lamps had been lit for some time that Zhuge Liang heard the distant clatter of horses' hooves gradually drawing near. He relaxed and smiled as he examined the roughly drawn topographical map lying before him in the flickering candlelight. He was an old hand at reading this kind of map, concentrating his attention on a few select areas. With a wave of the hand, he dismissed the map and returned swiftly to his room.

The next morning the sun had barely risen when Zhuge Liang left his room. Walking through the silent city along the narrow, desolate streets, he went out through the city gate and stood gazing into the distance at the flat wheat fields before him, and the narrow, yellow-earth post road that twisted and turned out of sight. This was the road that his armies had set out upon and the road that the speeding pony carrying the map had traversed the

night before. As he imagined, he met here a sweat-soaked scout horse, and listened in a calm and unruffled manner to the bad news that Ma Su had been unable to hold the garrison at Jieting. He walked slowly back through the city gate and climbed the gate tower. Meeting two old soldiers in the gateway he smiled faintly, making them wonder why the Prime Minister was happy today. He had not smiled like that since the time when Nanzhong was pacified, the allegiance of Meng Huo was won back and the troops had returned home in victory.

For a long time Zhuge Liang stood alone on the wall gazing into the distance.

Zhuge Liang felt with regret that the entire campaign was over. The long preparations had been cast aside for nothing. He felt ashamed. The deciding factor in his defeat had been the misuse of the chief commander of his forward contingent. There were difficulties ahead, but the major difficulties lay not in withdrawing his army and throwing off the pursuing armies of Sima Yi — this had been solved the evening before, and he calculated that losses could be cut down to a bare minimum. The greatest difficulty lay in problems that would arise after the army had retreated to Chuanzhong. How should he deal with Ma Su? And what about himself? He really had no way out. He could not resign, even less could he refuse to continue to direct the preparations for the expedition against the north. If he did not attack, he could only wait for the enemy to come and annihilate his army. How could he hold out and continue to rouse the fighting spirit of the people and army of Shu?

Zhuge Liang gazed into the deep blue sky. Would this place become a battlefield? Several past events suddenly flashed into his mind. Ma Su's fate had been determined very early with the first glance at that topographical map. What made Zhuge Liang so uneasy was the question of just who had pushed Ma Su into the deep waters of destruction and death? Was it Zhang He? After much thought he concluded it was the Prime Minister himself. The pallid face of Liu Bei seemed to appear before him in the snow. "Who told you to send in Ma Su as commander? How many times did I warn you that he cannot handle such a responsibility!" He could hear Liu Bei's weak but angry voice and see the red flush of agitation on the old man's face.

Zhuge Liang muttered something to himself that no one could understand. He was praying to the late emperor for help to get through this crisis and correct his mistakes. When he opened his eyes, the same expanse of brilliantly clear blue sky still lay before him.

Zhuge Liang instructed his attendants to order the old soldiers to sweep all the streets inside and outside the city gates and around the city walls. Then he ordered them to prepare some snacks to eat with wine and bring him his *qin*.* He had decided to drink a little, play his *qin* and admire the scenery. To his incredulous young attendant he explained: "Look! The scenery here is so beautiful. Look at that mountain...."

From the start, Zhuge Liang was prepared for the worst. He guessed that as soon as Sima Yi heard the news that Zhang He had seized Jieting, he would immediately assemble his forces and make a surprise attack on West City. This would take a minimum of two days. But he also considered the possibility of Sima Yi's arriving more

---

*The *qin* is a musical instrument resembling the zither.

quickly. He gazed off into the distance, but there was no sign of dust raised by horses' hooves. If he did arrive more quickly, what could be done anyway? Zhuge Liang suddenly felt a great surge of self-confidence. The depth of his understanding of Sima Yi far exceeded his knowledge of Ma Su. He felt little ashamed, but firmly believed that this time he would not make any more mistakes.

From the intelligence constantly being brought in by his scouts, Zhuge Liang knew that Sima Yi's troops were already advancing on West City. This news evoked quite different reactions from Zhuge Liang and from the small number of garrison troops left in the city. Zhuge Liang climbed slowly down the gate tower and met two old soldiers with whom he had once crossed the Lu River on an expedition south through Sichuan. He said, "You really must make an effort to sweep the town clean, the cleaner the better. Sweep this neighborhood to the left; there's no need to sweep those areas over there." He pointed with his fan towards tumbledown slums crowded into one corner of the city. A slight smile touched his face.

As it turned out, nothing exceeded Zhuge Liang's expectations, but he was not entirely correct either. Sima Yi's armies arrived even sooner than he had anticipated, even allowing a very high safety margin. A few crippled old soldiers had just finished cleaning up the streets around the left side of the city gate when a scout arrived to report: "Sima Yi's army is now close to West City!"

Zhuge Liang hastily reclimbed the gate tower, but no one could see any sign of anxiety in his mind. He sat like a scholarly eccentric on the city wall, drinking wine and playing his *qin*. Sima Yi knew all this in detail from his subordinates' reports, and the news made him inwardly alarmed. He reined his horse to halt on a small slope, still a long way from the city. He couldn't see clearly, but he was certain that the figure seated on the city wall could only be Zhuge Liang. He had had much experience of the world and knew that such a natural, unrestrained deportment and leisurely elegant manner of playing the *qin* could belong to no other man. This was the highest expression of the style and manner of the "Zhengshi" period of the Kingdom of Wei, and could hardly be imitated. Sima Yi hesitated for a long while on his horse and finally gave the order to retreat. He did not feel like taking part in Zhuge Liang's wine and music party. This was not the appropriate moment for a friendly get-together, and Zhuge Liang was not like to be a hospitable host. Sima Yi thought for a long time and finally made up his mind: "Go back."

Zhuge Liang sat in the hall looking highly agitated — a very rare sight. In the last two weeks he had acted out many roles. He had angrily punished Wang Ping, the deputy commander of the forward army, bringing into play the full weight of his anger, and had commended the veteran general Zhao Yun for covering the retreating army. But when the hatless and disheveled Ma Su was forced into the hall, his hands shackled and his face despondent, Zhuge Liang suddenly became calm. He knew that this was going to be his most critical trial.

Ma Su was like a defeated rooster in a cockfight. The proud and haughty air he had always worn in the past was gone. His voice was dull and hoarse. He admitted his guilt and accepted full responsibility, not even blaming his defeat on ill luck. This all made Zhuge Liang feel very vexed. If Ma Su had lost his temper and stressed the objective difficulties he had faced, it would have been easier to handle his case. But Ma Su was just not like. Zhuge Liang could only think that the whole tragedy was a trap into which he as Prime Minister had forced Ma Su. It was he who had wanted Ma Su to sign the military orders. Where had his famed insight into people's character and capabilities disappeared to?

The dignity of the military court faded from his mind and he rose from his seat and approached the kneeling man, intending to say a few words to him. Only then did he see that Ma Su's dispirited eyes were brimming with unshed tears. He forgot everything he was going to say. In deathly silence, the whole army officers and men stood ranked around him, every eye upon him, every ear strained to listen to his words. Then faintly at first, but soon louder and louder, wave after wave of suppressed murmuring broke the silence. Zhuge Liang was panic-stricken. This was the first time in his life he had lost his usual manner. His eyes swept the court room and he hastily escaped back to his seat. Quickly — one could even say perfunctorily — he issued the order for execution.

99

The Drunken Beauty

Yang Yuhuan was originally the consort of Prince Shou, a son of the Tang Emperor Minghuang. Emperor Minghuang discovered her beauty and first had her made a Taoist priestess and then afterwards took her into the palace to be the highest ranking imperial concubine, his favorite among 3,000.

This opera recounts the story of how Yang waited in the One Hundred Flower Pavilion for the emperor to arrive in order to drink with him.

When Mei Lanfang performed in this opera in the United States in the 1930s, his portrayal of the gestures and attitudes of the drunken concubine was so superbly convincing that it literally surpassed description, and was widely acclaimed by the American audiences and theater critics.

This opera is standby in the repertoire of actors in the Mei Lanfang school of Peking Opera. One need merely mention Peking Opera and people will immediately think of Mei Lanfang, and his most representative role is that of the tipsy concubine in the opera "The Drunken Beauty".

— Ed. —

Next to the Pavilion of Deep Fragrance, Gao Lishi watched attentively as the court maids laid out the banquet table, set pots of flowers about and prepared the wine, fruit and candles. He rushed around giving orders and continually whisking the ivory-handled duster in his hand. Though it was only the beginning of summer, beads of sweat covered his forehead.

It was the heyday of the Great Tang Empire. The country was at peace; its coffers and granaries were full; its frontiers were secure. Minghuang, the reigning emperor, spent nearly all of his time indulging in wine and women. Within the palace, it was festival delicacies morning after morning, New Year dumplings night after night, brocade and flowers everywhere. It seemed that the palace could no longer contain so many worldly pleasures, which would soon spill over the high walls into the world beyond. But for some unknown reason, Gao Lishi's thoughts were a bit cloudy. He fancies hearing a rumble of thunder from the direction of Taiye Pool; was a storm brewing?

The emperor had not wined or dined with Lady Yang Yuhuan, his favorite, for nearly two weeks. Of course, the reason for this was well known, but no one would mention it. Today, when the imperial concubine gave orders to prepare wine, her voice and manner were somewhat strange. Why was the rendezvous not being held in the palace but in this out-of-the-way pavilion? Gao Lishi did not like this place, for he had once made a fool of himself here; but he did not know that this was the very reason why Lady Yang had chosen the place. She hoped that the famous flowers and the pavilion and terrace would awaken the emperor's memories of the past — memories of good times spent together, the poem set to the song *Qingping Melody* that the great poet Li Bai wrote here, and the emperor's own words, "... enjoying the flowers face to face with my favorite...." The little lady had taken great pains in the petty feud that was now

102

going on; still, she could not be sure of the outcome.

Dressed in her finest gown and escorted by a procession of maids, the imperial concubine appeared on the scene sailing broadly; though nobody noticed the shadow that occasionally passed across her face. With an air of dignity, she looked at the flowers along the way; when passing over the Jade-and-Stone Bridge, she paused to observe the goldfish and the mandarin ducks as if all these things were very fresh and interesting. Slowly she approached the imperial table and sat down, at the same time casting a glance at the empty seat beside her and counseling herself to remain calm. The maids busied themselves with their tasks while Gao Lishi and Pei Lishi, eyes fixed upon the ground, stood in their places fixed by court etiquette. It was going to be a long, long wait for the arrival of His Majesty.

The day before, after court had adjourned, Lady Yang met the emperor in the palace and seized the opportunity to whisper to him her request for the banquet tonight in the Pavilion of Deep Fragrance. The emperor only smiled in silence. Of late, she had been much worried by this strange new expression on his face. She felt as if she had lost something and would never hold on to him again. She knew the cause of this change and hoped that through her initiative she could rekindle in his bosom the passion that was dying away. It was a risky venture, the outcome of which depended on whether or not he would appear tonight.

The bitter news arrived. The emperor would not be coming; his imperial carriage was headed for the West Palace, the residence of Lady Mei. Lady Yang lost her last reserves of dignity. She gave orders that she would have a few drinks by herself. She sought revenge. No longer caring about restoring the "face" she had lost, what she wanted was to lose even more. After all, the question of face and dignity was not her business alone; why should she try to resolve it by herself?

Though one of the two seats of honor that stood side by side was empty, the eunuchs and maids served up course after course in the prescribed manner. There were famous drinks like the Dragon-Phoenix Wine, so named because the emperor and his favorite had enjoyed it together. Now she was to drink it alone.

It was to be an all-night banquet at which the wine was to flow until dawn. But where was her drinking partner? At first she affected coyness and would hold up her fan to conceal the cup each time she put it to her lips; soon, however, she threw the fan aside and drank in huge gulps like a man; eventually she went so far as to snatch the cup from Gao Lishi's hands and pour the contents down her throat. The excess drinking made her feel hot and dry, and she stood up to remove her phoenix robe. She had only half risen when her legs weakened and she found she could hardly stand; but she held on to the table with one hand, smiled and shook her head at the maids who rushed up to help her. She was trying to cover up her incapacity for drink.

After removing her phoenix robe and putting on a court dress, Lady Yang turned to admire the flowers blooming in pots on the terrace. She wanted to smell the blossoms, but to do so she had to bend down. The eunuchs and maids watched with concern as she stooped, but none dared stop her or offer a hand. Seeing her with the bleary, half-closed eyes of one who had just walked out of a dream, they knew she was far gone. Yet when she turned around, she called for more wine.

Kneeling, the eunuchs and maids offered her a small cup on a gold platter. She bent down and sipped it; then, holding the cup between her teeth, she threw back her head and drained it to the last drop. She was dead drunk now, and leaning in a stupor against the balustrade, was soon in the land of dreams.

It was only last spring, at this very same pavilion, that amid peals of laughter she listened to the new poem composed to the tune of the *Qingping Melody*, and enjoyed watching "Third Brother Li" getting drunk. Now this was all a dream. "Third Brother Li" was the emperor's pet name which she dared to use only when she loved or hated him intensely. She recalled how she first caught the emperor's fancy in the home of Prince Shou. This was followed by unforgettable days of rejoicing. But today, for the first time, she realized how frail and insecure their love was; if the passionate love she had experienced could be passed on to another, what about the other favors that came along with it?

Time in dreams flies like an arrow: mountains can be crossed in one stride; and secular joys and sorrows, honor and dishonor, succeed each other in rapid sequence. Lady Yang felt as if she were riding an unbridled horse that was carrying her swiftly to the edge of a cliff. Just as she was about to call for help, she woke to find Gao Lishi and the others on their knees before her. Gently shaking her knees, they announced in a halting voice: "His Majesty is here!"

This was enough to dispel a good portion of her drunkenness and arouse her instantly. Hastily she clambered to her feet as the maids rushed up to help, fearing she would be unable to stand by herself. They escorted her to the flowered path and there, according to custom, prostrated themselves upon the ground. Lady Yang could not believe that what was happening was true; it had to be a dream! Burying her face in the long sleeves of her court dress, she crouched in shame and fear, not daring to lift her head and look at the emperor, who she imagined was standing before her.

Thus for quite some time she remained there on her hands and knees.

Finally a loyal attendant plucked up the courage to tell her that this was only a trick thought up by Gao Lishi and the others to revive her from her drunkenness. She was stunned. The sorry lot of eunuchs and maids that could hardly be called human were upon their knees again begging her forgiveness, but she stared at them blankly, sensing a sudden unbearable fatigue. The wine took effect again and she was about to collapse. Supported by her maids, she tottered back to her chambers.

It was almost midnight. In the stillness of the inner palace, the drums, flutes, and singing in the west court-yard sounded loud and clear. It was not the familiar *Rainbow and Feathery Garment Dance* they were playing; it was a new poem set to an old tune. Lady Yang in her drunken state did not notice it; but it fell upon the ears of Gao Lishi, vexing him slightly.

The Muke Mountain Redoubt

One of the characteristics of Peking Opera is that it features many historical romances which include numerous legends based on actual historical figures. Historically, there was indeed a man named Yang Jiye, the first of the generals of the Yang family. However, the stories concerning the patriotic exploits and love affairs of his descendants are merely the products of the imaginations of dramatists and authors.

This opera recounts the story of how, when Yang Yanzhao, a second generation general of the Yang family, led his troops to resist the Qidan (Khitan) invaders, Yang Zongbao, a third generation general of the Yang family, was captured by Mu Guiying, the daughter of a Song dynasty official who led a hermit's existence in the Muke Mountain Redoubt. Later, Yang Zongbao married Mu Guiying and together they went to the battle front to help repulse the Qidan invaders.

— Ed. —

The young woman general Mu Guiying appeared on the mountain slope, sitting erect upon her horse. She was a girl of about 17 or 18 years old and wore a full suit of armor. The banners she wore on her back fluttered in regular rows that stretched in all directions. As she looked around, surveying the grasslands and forests below her feet, a lively expression lit up her face. She had come out today to divert herself by going hunting, so she need not have worn her full military battle attire; but she loved to dress up this way anyway.

The servant girl by her side cried out, "Mistress, the geese are coming!" Mu Guiying followed the path of the wild geese that flew across the sky. She took up her carved bow, grasped it with her left hand, and drew back the arrow with her right. She fired and immediately struck a direct hit. The injured goose flew on with the arrow stuck in its belly, and they spurred their horses forward to follow it.

General Mu Guiying did not command the army of any ordinary country: she was the daughter of the ruler of a fortified mountain city. During the Northern Song dynasty, fortified cities of this type could be found almost everywhere. The majority of them were occupied by peasants who had fled in desperation from intolerable taxation and oppression, though they also provided a haven for dismissed court officials.

Mu Hongju, Guiying's father, was the master of the fortified city of Muke. He himself had previously been an official of the Song court, but evil and treacherous ministers had forced him to flee and hide in the forest. To speak more truthfully, he had forcefully occupied the mountain territory and made himself its ruler. His family consisted of his one daughter whom he loved dearly, and who possessed uncommon skills in the arts of war and in commanding an army, besides numerous other remarkable abilities. The aging ruler had handed over most of the "affairs of state" into her capable hands. As for the headstrong yet intelligent character of his daughter, the old master could do little to change that. His love for his daughter at times became almost obsessive. But the old man was no fool, and knew that although his daughter was young and had little experience of the world, she had a pure heart and was honest and upright in her dealings with others. He said, "She would never take a step in the wrong direction." He could rely on her with his mind at ease. Indeed, even now, he had left the mountain to go traveling.

As Mu Guiying galloped on her horse across the mountainside, she noticed in the far distance two war horses and two generals standing on the grass plain in full battle dress. One of them had a face as red as a ball of fire — this was Meng Liang; the other had a face as black as the bottom of a cooking pot — this was Jiao Zan. They were sworn brothers of Yang Yanzhao, the commander-in-chief of the garrison of the Three Passes.

It was they who had picked up the wild goose shot by Mu Guiying. Meng Liang took the arrow that Jiao Zan had plucked from the dead goose, and carefully inspected the words that were finely carved into its shaft: "One hundred arrows fired by Mu Guiying gain one hundred direct hits."

"This is Mu Guiying's arrow!" exclaimed Meng Liang. It was precisely in order to see Mu Guiying that their commander had sent them here. They had come to request her to give them the "dragon-subduing wood".

At that time, war had once more broken out between the kingdoms of Song and Liao (Qidan). Xiao Tianzuo, from the Kingdom of Liao, was organizing the army battalions, while Yang Yanzhao went throughout the land seeking troop reinforcements and asking retired generals to take up arms once more. Yang also ordered Jiao Zan to go to Wutai Mountain to ask his fifth brother, who had become a monk, to lend his assistance. Commander Yang's fifth brother wanted to use the "dragon-subduing wood" to make the handle of his broad ax. This therefore was the mission that had brought these two brothers to such distant lands, for the special "dragon-subduing wood" was the treasured asset of this strategic mountain city.

The two brothers discussed how to dispose of the arrow that was now in their possession. Meng Liang opined that they should give both the arrow and the goose back to their rightful owner; but Jiao Zan proposed that they should use this opportunity to bargain more effectively with Mu Guiying. He seized the arrow and said, "The 'dragon-subduing wood' will be ours for sure!"

At this moment, Mu Guiying's servant girl approached to reclaim the goose. When Jiao Zan saw that it was not Mu Guiying herself who had come, he cried out, "Go back and tell Mu Guiying to provide us with the 'dragon-subduing wood'. If she refuses, we will destroy your mountain city!" This provoked a fight between them, but in the end, the servant girl lost and went away.

Mu Guiying then came over in person, whereupon Jiao Zan pulled Meng Liang onto his horse. Judging that this situation should not be dealt with by force, Meng Liang blurted out "Miss Mu . . ." but was quickly silenced by Jiao Zan. Jiao Zan did not consider such politeness necessary; instead, he came straight to the point and simply repeated what he had said to the servant girl. Instantly, another battle ensued. But this time, the outcome was different, for it was the brothers who were knocked off their horses and defeated. After her victory, Mu Guiying rode back into the mountains.

The order to go to Muke had originally come down from the supreme commander to Jiao Zan alone. But along the way, Jiao Zan chanced to meet up with Meng Liang, who was returning to his garrison to report in, and the two of them continued on together.

In the eyes of Jiao Zan, Meng Liang was sometimes rather faint-hearted and overcautious and could not compare with himself in terms of intelligence and flexibility. Unfortunately, he had under-estimated Mu Guiying this time. "Two formidable generals were pulled off our horses by that young slip of a girl. What a disgrace!" Jiao Zan could say nothing in reply to the angry reprimands of Meng Liang. But then he came up with a plan: without informing his supreme commander, he asked Yang Zongbao to come and lend a hand. He was sure that the combined force of three cavaliers would suppress that girl bandit once and for all! The young general Yang Zongbao, at the time under orders to inspect the garrison and the sentry posts, was hence persuaded by the two brothers to come and help them out.

Mu Guiying's eyes lit up at the apparition before her. She had never in her life seen such a dashing and magnificent young man as General Yang Zongbao, mounted as he was on a white horse with a silver spear at his side. Although Mu Guiying was the daughter of a so-called "King of Heaven", and had practiced the arts of war with her father since childhood, she had never strayed too far from her mountain home to explore the bustling world around her. She understood nothing of the rules of etiquette and had certainly never met any man of outstanding qualities. Yang Zongbao reminded her of the statue of Skanda holding his demon-defying club, which stood in front of the temple she visited with her father when she was a child. Surely this was none other than the reincarnation of Skanda himself, riding down the mountainside. When their two horses met, Mu Guiying scrutinized this young general from head to toe. She asked him his name and the purpose of his journey. When she learned that he was Commander Yang's son, and that he had come to fetch "dragon-subduing wood", she exclaimed: "Very well! Leave it all up to me. Come up the mountainside and get them!"

They fought as they rode on horseback. But Mu Guiying did not fight as she had with Meng Liang and Jiao Zan. This combat was much less violent; and the outcome was predictable before they started. As Mu Guiying intercepted Yang Zongbao's lunging silver spear, she was seeking a way to size up her opponent more carefully and ask him a few questions. He was a truly courageous young general, but he appeared to understand very little about human feelings. He had hardly noticed that his enemy was a girl. For an instant, the venom would rise up in her and she would close in upon him, driving him back. But she had no wish to injure him and simply gave him a long look, as if to say: "How could you be in such fury!" and then purse her lips in a smile and pull her horse around.

Yang Zongbao was also rather perplexed by this situation, for he could hardly tell if his young opponent was fighting or simply play-acting. She attacked with great ferocity, yet always seemed to draw back at the critical moment. He gathered all his courage and made a secret resolve; this time he would knock her off her horse once and for all. But once again, their fighting resulted in a draw. Yang Zongbao was quite unaware of the purposeful restraint being practiced by his opponent; at

the same time, he was roused to anger by her vicious parries.

By this time, Mu Guiying had worked out a plan of action. She led the young general up the mountain slope and once more fought him into a tough corner. She grabbed his silver spear and lightly jerked it upward, tumbling Yang Zongbao off his horse. Thereupon, the assistant at her side came forward and with a well-practiced hand tied up the prisoner. She then raised him onto the back of his horse and took him back to the fortified mountain city.

Jiao Zan and Meng Liang cried out in dismay as they watched the scene from their mountain hiding place. Jiao Zan was still unwilling to admit defeat. Pointing to the "fire gourd" Meng Liang was carrying on his back, he suggested they should burn the whole mountain to ashes. He claimed to be able to "direct the flames" and that by chanting magic incantations he could summon up an "iee dragon", which he would then ride into the flames and rescue Yang Zongbao.

They set the mountain on fire, but Mu Guiying herself possessed a "flame dividing fan", with which she fanned Jiao Zan and Meng Liang right into the fire, burning their faces black and singeing away their eyebrows and whiskers. They had no choice but to pick up their burning hot weapons and return to their garrison in disgrace.

Yang Paifeng

In the story of how the four generations of generals of the Yang family defended the nation, many women in the family play an important role. The bravery and resourcefulness of such Yang family heroines as She Saihua, Yang Bajie (Sister Number Eight), Princess Chai and Mu Guiying exceeded that of male generals who struck terror into the hearts of the enemy. Even Yang Paifeng, a maidservant in the Yang household who was responsible for tending the hearth and serving tea, was also a warrior skilled in the martial arts.

The main purpose of this play is to give the protagonist Yang Paifeng a chance to display her skill in fighting. Although it recounts a tale of war and strife, the opera is full of humor and invariably delights its audiences.

— Ed. —

When Yang Paifeng returned after rendering meritorious service at the Three Passes, she resumed her old work of tending the fires in the great kitchen of the Tianbo Palace. In accordance with the orders issued by Yang Zongbao's mother, whoever rescued Yang Zongbao from the border region, where he had been captured by the Liao general Han Chang, and returned him to court would "assume a high office and ride a magnificent steed". Yang Paifeng deserved to have a grand title conferred upon her, but she rejected the honor in favor of returning to tend the kitchen fires in the belief that she would be more at ease with work she was familiar with.

She was employed in the palace of the venerable Mrs. Yang since her childhood and worked in the kitchen, where the poker never left her hand throughout the day. After her glorious return, it was this poker that became famous as the Black Dragon Cudgel. In her idle moments she would play with the poker, creating new fighting techniques. Both male and female generals lived in the Tianbo Palace, and swordplay was as common an occurrence there as drinking tea. Merely by watching, even the most dim-witted person would be able to pick up some of their martial arts skills. Not a soul knew of Yang Paifeng's ability, not even Mrs. Yang. Most people thought of her as a mischievous young girl. How very right they were!

After returning from the Three Passes, Paifeng's status in the household changed. Although she hadn't been granted an official post, when she walked by men would glance at her with strange expressions. This wasn't jealousy, since with no official post she had nothing to arouse their envy, but all the same they felt she was a curiosity, and were even embarrassed to enquire about her. Her young sisters in the kitchen began to pester her for stories of her fight with Han Chang whenever the opportunity presented itself.

"What can I say? There was no exchange of blows; I merely struck him on the head, struck him on the waist, and swept his horse from under him. Then he ran away! Don't be taken in by overbearing generals who sit high in the saddle — they're all quite useless. So what is there to tell? It was just like tending the fires at home. Nothing to get excited about." Paifeng sat there frowning and refused to say another word.

All the girls who were listening also found her story quite devoid of interest.

It was only when the name Jiao Zan was mentioned that Paifeng began to smile, though no one understood why. She thought to herself: "It was so difficult getting involved in the first place. Beating Han Chang was easy, but going into battle and fighting him was really difficult."

On that day, Meng Liang had returned flustered and desperate from the frontier passes to report the battle situation to Mrs. Yang, and suggested that officers be appointed. Mrs. Yang explained the situation to her men, stipulating the ranks and rewards to be given to successful warriors. For a long time, the officers filing the courtyard waited without a sound. "This isn't the custom of the Tianbo Palace," Paifeng remonstrated. "It was I who squeezed my way out from behind the crowd of people, eager to fulfill the pressing task. When Meng Liang saw me, he laughed and called me a little girl. And when Mrs. Yang saw me, she also refused to believe I had any ability. You don't know how difficult it was. There were more than twenty leading generals there in the Three Passes, none of them a match for Han Chang; how could a 'little girl' hope to succeed?

"Generals are selected from the most talented soldiers. Since the Tianbo Palace generals were defeated by Han Chang, does this mean that there are no men of talent here? Can a slave girl who attends the fires be considered a person of talent? My Black Dragon Cudgel, stained by smoke and singed by fire, can hardly compare with the knives and spears stored in the armory, so it's not surprising that Meng Liang laughed. His appraisal of me

118

was: 'On a horse she's no bigger than my fist; dismounted she barely comes up to my knees. As for going into battle, she could hardly withstand the dull edge of a sword or a horse's kick.' Meng Liang cannot be blamed for considering my appearance alone; he is getting on in years, and already has a long beard. Although he himself has little ability, he is sincere and kindly nevertheless, and always corrects his errors when he becomes aware of them. When he was testing my fighting skills in the flower garden, I knocked his weapons out of his hands within seconds, and had him crawling on the ground. He is a man who knows how to acknowledge defeat. He endured my cudgel and admitted he was wrong; then in front of Mrs. Yang he did all he could to ensure I would go to the Three Passes — this is his good side. In the end, General Meng does have the demeanor of a great general. Of course, a great general has to rely on his own abilities; but he must also rely on his judgment to recognize men of ability, and not refuse to admit mistakes in the face of facts. If he bets and loses, he must apologize, even to the little girl who tends the fires. This was understandably a very embarrassing loss of face for him. Just look how he turns away in shame. . . ." Yang Paifeng couldn't suppress a giggle. "Ah! This was the first pass I broke through."

"Meng Liang led me to the Three Passes where I saw Commander Yang. But from there I still had to make my way through two more passes before meeting Han Chang face to face. The last two passes I stormed were really no different from the first pass I had broken through at the Tianbo Palace. Normally, with Mrs. Yang's orders and Meng Liang's guarantee, Commander Yang should have believed in me, but he failed to. He assessed me in the same manner as Meng Liang. They had to test me, to

weigh me in the palms of their own hands: You can believe your eyes, but not necessarily believe your ears.

"A supreme commander must have the dignity of a supreme commander. He may not disobey his mother's orders, but now he half-believes and half-doubts. This is pardonable, for the weight of responsibility that lies on his shoulders is indeed heavy. But Commander Yang is wily; he supported Jiao Zan when testing me in competition, and himself stood as guarantor. Should Jiao Zan win, he would be justified in sending me back to Mrs. Yang. But if he lost it would do no damage to his own reputation.

"Jiao Zan really is the limit! He too is one of the star generals of the Three Passes. Meng Liang had a great red face, but Jiao Zan's face was as black as the bottom of a cooking pot. He looks like he has just pulled his head out of the kitchen stove. He is less honest and tolerant than Meng Liang, though he is thoughtful and circumspect. When all is said and done, he's still a good man, faithful and true. It's just that he's rather careless in handling his affairs. When Yang Zongbao visited the grave of his grand father, the old supreme commander, to plant a willow, it was Jiao Zan who set off a firecracker and aroused Han Chang, whereupon the Liao soldiers captured him.

"Right at the start, Jiao Zan asked Meng Liang: 'How many soldiers are being transferred here and how many generals?' He never imagined that it was only me, a girl who tended the fires. When I saw him, I couldn't help but laugh. He was the spitting image of a first rate army cook. Unexpectedly, Jiao Zan sized me up and began to laugh as well. What is strange is that his words were identical to those of Meng Liang at the Tianbo Palace.

"Meng Liang not only urged Jiao Zan to compete with me, but also made a bet and entrusted Commander Yang to act as guarantor. He enjoined me to use all of my skills in the arena and told me that he would take responsibility for any accidents. At this time there is no need to mention that Jiao Zan and the Commander Yang were both very suspicious. Only Meng Liang was sure of what he was doing. But to say that he was deliberately playing a dirty trick in order to fool Jiao Zan is not true either. Jiao Zan is stubborn. The best way to convince him is to allow him to learn for himself. The three of them are sworn brothers, well aware of each other's temperament. Meng Liang knows that Jiao Zan must be made to traverse the path that he himself has already taken. Mere words will not suffice.

"Before we engaged in conflict, I first saluted Jiao Zan: 'General Jiao, should I strike you by a slip of the hand, pray do not blame me.' Hearing this he became flustered and began to stutter. I pretended to be losing and let him preserve a little of his self-respect. By the time Commander Yang led Meng Liang to the arena, Jiao Zan had long since been crawling on the ground, unable to get up."

Yang Paifeng left the Tianbo Palace and arrived at the Three Passes where she defeated Han Chang and rescued Yang Zongbao. To her, this difficult venture was as easy as taking a trip to the temple fair. In fact, it required very little effort for her to beat Han Chang. But for a girl who tends the fires to even think of strapping on armor and entering into battle is no mean achievement. She broke through the three passes by using her cudgel as well as her intelligence and charm. She never forgot those good men, Meng Liang, Jiao Zan and Commander Yang.... She smiled when she thought of what she had to go through to convince these good men to let her go into battle. It was as if she had to surmount a thousand difficulties in order to attend a temple fair.

The Fisherman's Revenge

Like other Chinese operas, the opera "The Fisherman's Revenge" is also known by other names, in this case "Qingding Pearl" and "Collecting the Fishing Tax". This item is frequently included in the repertoire of Peking Opera, Hanju (Hubei Opera), and Qinqiang (Shaanxi Opera).

When the celebrated Peking Opera master Mei Lanfang performed in this opera in the United States and the Soviet Union during the 1930s he used an oar to skillfully pantomime the motions of a girl frantically paddling a small boat bobbing in midstream. The German dramatist Bertolt Brecht cited this performance in comparing the differences between the system of performance in Chinese opera and that of the school of acting founded by the Soviet dramatist Stanislavski.

This opera, which has enjoyed popularity in China for many years, tells the story of a poor but honest fisherman, who, getting into a conflict with a brutal and greedy local despot, slays him and is forced to flee for his life.

— Ed. —

The weather had been sunny and clear for more than half a month, since summer time began. Every family in this fishing village took advantage of the fine weather to mend their nets at the river shore. The water in the river had dropped so low that the bowl-sized round pebbles emerged from the water, and spread about the shore. Fishermen erected sturdy bamboo poles along the shore and hung their fishing nets on them. Most of those mending the nets were old men and young women. No young men participated in this work. While they worked, they carried on exhilarating conversations about trifling events which had occurred in the village, punctuating their tales with merry laughter. Before any of them noticed, night had fallen, and as the flaming sun edged its way over the western hills, the villagers started gathering their nets and set out on their way home for dinner.

The river glistened in fish-scale patterns of golden light, and a vast expanse of red clouds were reflected in the river in crimson. Rows of weeping willow trees, a good number of which grew in the water, revealed their dark water-soaked trunks. With their twisted branches, they appeared both strong and stubborn. Beneath the shade of the willows, a little boat was tied up at the bank of the river, as if it were trying to escape from the crowd. Two people sat in the boat, a father and his daughter; silently, they arranged their fishing spears and nets. On the floor of the boat's cabin lay a dozen small fishes, the fruits of a half-day's work.

"Father," the girl noticed how tired her father was from the expression on his face, and tried to say something, but finally remained silent. When the old man turned around, you could see that his carelessly shaven sideburns visible under his straw hat were white, though his eyes still shone with a penetrating fire, he hardly looked like a common fisherman. Glancing at his daughter, he noticed her woven straw hat, concealing a head of beautiful thick black hair put up in a bun, and a wild flower she had inserted behind her ear. The old man's glance softened, and he went back to the work at hand.

"Guiying, please tidy up the fish, I'm going to drink two jugs of wine."

"Father, after half a day's hard work, we only have fish to bring us a few pennies; how can we ever go on live this...." the girl replied to him.

"But what else could we do if we don't catch fish?"

Xiao En realized that he was talking crudely again, which was one of his old weaknesses. For years he had been restraining himself in an effort to appear like a properly behaved old man in front of other people. But in company with his own daughter, his "bad old manner" could occasionally reappear unconsciously. But whenever this happened, he always felt guilty and annoyed.

Guiying picked up the fish in silence, and walked to the boat's rear cabin.

"Dad, someone is calling you from the river bank!" she yelled from the rear cabin.

Xiao En was suddenly shaken from his musing, and heard someone calling him from afar. Squinting in the direction of the voices, he saw Li Jun and a middle-aged stranger standing on the bank. It had been long since any of his old friends had come to visit him, so Xiao En was very happy to see them.

In their small village, the Xiao family was quite isolated from their neighbors. Though they had little contact with the other villagers, people knew that he was an old man of kind temper, and that his young daughter never played with the other girls. Nobody knew much about the old man's background; from the way they earned their keep, it seemed unlikely that they came from a long line of fishermen. Since they rarely had any grests,

Li Jun's sudden visit was the source of much unexpected happinesses for Xiao En.

Xiao En welcomed his guests on board the boat. The stranger followed Li Jun onto the bow of the boat, but his foot slipped, and only Xiao En's steady grasp prevented him from falling into the water. Li Jun used this opportunity to introduce them.

"What strong arms you have, my good man!" Ni Rong could tell that Xiao En was not a man of a common strength.

"I am old and useless!" Xiao En joked while glancing at Li Jun. He imagined that Li Jun could have told Ni Rong about his past, so he felt no need to hold anything back. He introduced his daughter to them and announced her fiance's name — Hua Fengchun, who was the son of Hua Rong.

"A good match!" the guests said simultaneously, and laughed at each other.

Though their meeting was fleeting and their conversation brief, they already felt like intimate friends. To celebrate, Xiao En instructed his daughter to set out wine cups, and the host and guests sat down at the narrow bow of the boat. Although Xiao En was by nature a solemn man, he suggested they play a drinking game. The words "dry" and "drought" were taboo among fishermen, and if anyone said either of these words while drinking, they would have to drink three cups of wine as punishment. They drank their first toast as they continued to talk and joke. Ni Rong lifted his empty wine cup to Xiao En, and said, "Bottom's up", which is a homonym of "dry". Xiao En smiled and filled up his cup again. In the meantime, Ni Rong noticed someone peering stealthily into the rear cabin. He put his hand on the top of his cup and said:

"Brother Xiao there's someone on the bank!"

Xiao En leapt off the boat and gave directions to a suspicious-looking passer-by who had lost his way, after which he returned to the cabin silently. When Ni Rong heard it was someone asking the way, he blurted out, "Asking the way? He's obviously...." "He wouldn't dare!" Li Jun interrupted in order to silence Ni Rong. Xiao En remained silent, though there was something on his mind he was having trouble keeping to himself. "When can I get away from this repugnant place?" Xiao En thought. Actually, he had been thinking this way for quite a long time. It was years since they first arrived incognito in this village, and the young girl had grown up by now. The old man didn't want his daughter to become a fisherman, and he always hoped that she would run away and live an entirely different kind of life. This all seemed like a dream now, which left the old man harboring guilty conscience about the fate of his only daughter.

Li Jun put his wine cup down and told his host that he had drunk enough.

Again there was a voice calling for Xiao En. This time it was a group of underlings from the Ding mansion who had come to press for payment of the fishing tax. Li Jun and Ni Rong heard the whole conversation from where they sat. This so-called fishing tax was neither a tax imposed by the state nor was it anything legal in the first place, rather, it was a sum of money extorted by the local tyrant Ding.

This "news" both startled and upset them. But beyond that they couldn't understand why Xiao En answered them in such a polite tone of voice.

"The weather has been very dry, and the water level is quite low, so our catch has been quite small. But as soon as we have the money, we will submit it to you."

The runners from the Ding mansion finally left after being appeased by Xiao En's flattering words, but Li Jun and Ni Rong called them back. The two of them were so upset with Xiao En's behavior that they criticized him, "How can you put up with these types?"

"They outnumber us, though."

"But we have a lot of people on our side as well."

"They've got a lot of influence in this area."

"We can't put up with this kind of cheating and oppression for long!"

Though they seemed to be having trouble agreeing on anything, Li Jun and Ni Rong told the underlings forward a message to the county officers to repeal the fishing tax or else "something inconvenient might befall them!" These were Li Jun's words, but when it came to Ni Rong's turn, he said, "If we meet in the street, we'll peel off their skin, extract their muscles, and dig out their eyes to soak them in wine and swallow them!"

Xiao En wanted to make peace, but he knew he couldn't hold back the rising tide. He also knew that when these runners returned they would spice their complete report with a number of inflammatory details, which would only lead to more trouble. But, on the other hand, he took pleasure in the fact that these friends seemed to bring him back to the old days. There was no doubt that they had "a lot of people on their side". The last few years, he had become accustomed to stooping in compromise and behaving according to rules.

But, today, he felt he was realizing the old dream he forgotten for years. After seeing his old friends off, the fisherman and his daughter cleared away the dishes and cups, cast off the line, and slowly swung the little boat towards home. Like in a dream, a faint smile played on Xiao En's face for the duration of the journey.

"Father, who were those two uncles?" The young girl was both interested in and excited about the meeting that had just taken place. She wondered how her father could have friends like them, and she was also puzzled by the fact that her father was in such a good mood, since he had not even smiled to himself for a long time.

"Ah, yes, those friends of mine." Xiao En rowed without stopping, his face turned towards the sunset. He spoke as if in a dream, "They, they are the wandering

heroes of the rivers and lakes, good friends of mine. They
had everything it took to become high officials, to wear
officials' robes, and to ride on fine horses, but they gave it
all up in favor of a life of wandering among the rivers and
lakes, what's more they didn't forget their old friend.
They are true friends...."

His voice was slow and soft; the little boat floating
gently through the water, the sound of the paddle
breaking the water was hurried but harmonious, a fitting
accompaniment for the old man's soliloquy. All of a

sudden, a flock of water birds flew up from a thicket of reeds; they seemed to be heading for the crystalline full moon, hanging in the sky.

Master Ding was sitting in a dignified fashion in his mansion. Ding had a square face, large ears, and a full nearly round forehead. Since it was his custom to sit all day long on the "great master's chair" in the center of the hall, he did very little exercise and hardly exposed himself to the sun. Thus his face was pale; his four limbs appeared somewhat feeble. But in the eyes of the local countrymen, Master Ding's appearance was awe-inspiring.

People in Ding's position were called "countryside officials", since at some time in the past they had held a job in the court, and after retiring and returning to the countryside, they still maintained a modicum of power. The new officers who had just been assigned official posts in the town came regularly to pay homage to these retired officers. In this way, they would become close companions and be able to rely on each other's prestige and power to facilitate their engaging in all sort of profitable businesses. The fishing tax was just one of their creations which lay outside of the law. Their method was as follows: in order not to become involved with the ordinary people directly they hired a private adviser to scheme and organize, and provided him with servants to do the dirty work. In addition, a group of armed "hatchet men" were hired to guard their mansions. Their end goal was to force the country folk to obey the rules they made without creating any major disturbances.

The underlings returning from the river reported the details of Xiao En's refusal to pay taxes. Master Ding listened with great interest, and asked his private adviser to write down the names of the two visitors — "Wandering Dragon" and "Curly-Haired Tiger". How can honest people have such nicknames? Although Xiao En hadn't said anything bad, he did make friends with a bandit gang, which removed all doubts as to his honesty. The adviser tacitly understood what his master wanted, and decided to work along two lines: he would bring the underlings with him to Xiao En's boat and denounce him for his complicity; at the same time, he would inform the county yamen to keep a close watch on any untoward developments. With "Wandering Dragon" and "Curly-Haired Tiger" around, they could not afford to lower their guard. Their presence signaled an upcoming storm.

Xiao En's mind was in a turmoil. Although he had hardly tested his drinking capacity, the night before with Li Jun and Ni Rong, he had gotten drunk slightly, which he saw as a sign of senility. He also dreamt many confusing dreams. Li Jun and Ni Rong had urged him to quit the fisherman's life, and promised to give him financial support. This moved him deeply, but would this allow him to live a peaceful life? Li Jun and Ni Rong's vulgar words had already sown the seeds of disaster, since he knew they embellished the truth to a point where even his flattery would do no good.

Xiao En decided to forget about it, but the thought of his daughter Guiying was grown up now returned to upset him. For the last ten years, they had relied on each other to survive; how could they separate now? Though she had grown to more and more like a fisherman's daughter, her father knew she couldn't live in this fishing village forever. . . .

Xiao En rose from his bed, put on his coat, opened the thatched door of his hut, and started pacing back and forth in his front yard, looking up at the sky from time to time. After a few minutes, he returned to his hut and sat down. Seeing that father was up, Guiying made a cup of tea and brought it over to him. Xiao En glanced at his daughter's long, thin fingers, and from there to her wrists. She was smartly dressed and wore an elegant straw hat which shaded her sweet smiling face. At this moment, a strong feeling of dejection rose in Xiao En's heart, and he heaved a deep sigh.

"Your mother died when you were young, and your father doesn't know how to take care of you. You dress just like a fisherman!"

"What's wrong with that? We live in a fishing village, we work as fishermen, so it's only natural we dress like fishermen." Guiying fondled the wild flower in her hair, and was about to say something, but held herself back when she noticed the old man's stern glance. She could not understand why her father was so upset about her wearing fishermen's clothing, but since she hated getting him upset, she said, "I won't go against my father's wishes," and with pouting lips, she went to the back room.

"Xiao En!" somebody shouted from outside. Guiying rushed to open the door, but was restrained by Xiao En. He heard several people speaking outside.

The chief body guard at Ding's mansion was named "Left Brass Cudgel", he was hired for a fat sum of money, and provided with a group of underlings. His main duty was to "guard the mansion and protect the courtyards", or to be more specific, to shut up the gates of the mansion and drill his underlings in the "martial arts", including boasting, drinking and sleeping. Besides this "mansion" and its "courtyards" there was no need to deal with anything outside of the gate. The special trip today was the result of his agreeing with the private adviser to take on the responsibility. The private adviser made sure to promise him that this was a one-shot deal. "Left Brass Cudgel" had heard that Xiao En was an old nuisance who generally knew his place. He lingered around until the sun was setting in the west before heading for Xiao En's house and only brought ten or so underlings with him.

Noticing that the thatched door of Xiao En's was closed, the body guard decided that nobody was at home, and ordered his underlings to return. But, after his underlings pointed out that the door was not locked and that there were fishing nets hanging about, he concluded that the owner was at home. Unable to decide who was going to open the door, Left Brass Cudgel volunteered to give a demonstration. He stood in front of the thatched door, assumed the proper position for battering down doors, and stretched out one of his arms as straight as a rod. As he imparted the essentials to his disciples, he said, "If he doesn't come out then forget it. But the moment he emerges, I'll bash him on and kick him around till he can't get up!" His body quivered for a moment as his eyes narrowed in a squint. In the meantime, Xiao En had opened the door, and before he knew it, Cudgel was swept off his feet and found himself sitting on the ground.

"Who's there?" Xiao En said as he peered out the door. The chief was helped to his feet by his underlings, and saw clearly that Xiao En was but a crotchety old man. The iron chain used to shackle criminals that Cudgel had brought with him was the so-called "law of the land" which by his own explanation was "what your grandma put around your neck when you were a child to serve as a good luck charm and prevent evil spirits from running off with your young soul". After a long discussion, they concluded that this old fellow was as sticky as tabby the way he hemmed and hawed about paying his taxes, and decided to "invite" him for a visit to the Ding mansion. Cudgel said, "When you see the chain hanging around his neck, you can drag him away!"

Concealing the "law of the land" behind his back, Left Brass Cudgel approached Xiao En and said, "Since you say you don't have any money to pay your taxes, do you recognize this?" He whipped out the chain, but in a flash Xiao En had managed to loop the chain over Cudgel's neck. And when the chief watchman's underlings pulled on it as they started to run, it was Cudgel who stumbled and was dragged to the side of the road.

Cudgel cursed his underlings for catching him in the chain, but they replied somewhat sarcastically that the

"law of the land" must have found its way around his neck for a reason? After further discussion, they decided that Xiao En was a formidable opponent, and that they would be more li ly to succeed if they used softer tactics.

The Cudgel walked up to Xiao En and giggled nervously in a way at made him sound like a happy goat.

"Xiao En, a wise man like yourself should know that we come here to collect the fishing tax only because we are under orders. Let's forget about the money business, you come with us to see our master. That way you can deal with him directly. How's that?"

Xiao En remained calm when dealing with them. But, if he could not choose his fate, the important thing was to hold himself steady. He was not afraid of Cudgel so much as the people who backed Xiao En up. It turned out that what Li Jun and Ni Rong said was actually the cause of this trouble. They had tried both hard and soft tactics, what would try next? Xiao En could see he was being driven to the edge of the river. That he would have to jump in seemed inevitable, though he struggled with the hope of remaining on the bank.

"This sounds very nice, but, unfortunately..." Xiao En restrained his rising resentment and tried to figure out a way of refusing this "invitation". "This particular old man doesn't have time," he muttered.

"Neither soft words nor hard blows seem to work," Cudgel also felt that he had come to the end of his tether.

At the thought of a fight, Xiao En's spirits were stirred up, and he felt a sudden sense of relief. He thought back on his youth, and couldn't help but smile.

"When this particular old fellow was a boy, whenever I heard about a fight, I would become as happy and excited as if I had been given a new pair of shoes for the New Year! But now I am old, and barely able to fight anymore." Xiao En was still struggling to hold himself back.

Xiao En's words were of no avail, and they fought at last. The underlings swiftly fled, leaving Cudgel to face Xiao En alone. Xiao En stopped fighting. He was acting as cruel as a cat, which had caught a mouse. Rather than eat it up right away, he leisurely and maliciously proceeded to watch it struggle, and shiver on the brink of death. Xiao En enjoyed himself thoroughly, until Guiying drove Cudgel away with one blow of a bamboo pole.

"Father, wasn't that a beautiful hit?" Guiying said.

"A good job indeed!" Xiao En said. "But the worst is yet to come."

Xiao En was exhausted but because he had just fought and won. Compared to all the battles he had fought during his lifetime, this minor confrontation hardly added up to anything at all. Nevertheless, he felt drained of all his energy. At first he had tried to keep his feelings to himself, but he ended up calling them a "bunch of lackeys", the likes of which he had never seen before. There were heroes who drove away tigers, but rarely heroes who devoted their energies to such contemptible "dogs".

Looking at his smiling daughter, Xiao En could only sigh.

"What are we going to do now, Father?" Guiying said.

Xiao En remained silent and held out his hand. When Guiying timidly handed him the bamboo pole, he cleared his throat and said, "Foolish child!"

Xiao En asked his daughter to bring him the clothing he wore when he went to town, and told her he was going to the county yamen office to file a lawsuit. "Father, you look tired. Why don't you wait till tomorrow?"

"I must go now. Tomorrow may be too late."

The old man took the neatly folded overcoat from her, and she watched her father step out of the door and head towards the river bank without glancing back.

Guiying was all alone. For the rest of the afternoon, she didn't feel like tidying up the room of preparing dinner. As if she were dreaming she saw her father cross the river, enter the yamen office and tell his story before the court. The judge had a kind, round face, and asking him about details of the case, offered a few comforting words, and announced that the fishing tax was repealed. Guiying closed her eyes, and her face beamed with a peaceful smile. When she suddenly opened her eyes, their little yard was flooded with the light of the sunset. She went out to gaze at the river, but their little boat was still nowhere to be seen. The river was as calm as a mirror, without the shadow of a single boat. Later that night, the door opened suddenly, and Xiao En walked in, out of breath and barely able to stand on his own two feet. Guiying rushed to take her father's coat and he fell right into his daughter's arms.

Guiying listened with astonishment to her father's story. Quite the opposite to what she had dreamed, the judge, without asking a single question, no sooner opened his mouth than ordered Xiao En to be dragged out and beaten. After being struck fourty times with a paddle, he was tossed out into the street.

Guiying started to cry. She stared silently at her father's angry mien, not knowing what to say. She was

thoroughly familiar with the old man's temper: burning oil cannot be extinguished with water, no more than he was open to persuasion.

A moment later, Xiao En murmured, "And, that's not all!"

In a fit of terror, Guiying grabbed the old man's shoulders and shook them hard.

"After I was beaten, that scoundrel of a judge ordered me to apologize to that old bastard Ding!" Xiao En spoke as if he were in an empty hall, and relaxed as if he were telling a story.

"Father, do you really have to cross the river again?"

"Of course!" A hideous grin appeared on his face. "I can't wait any longer. If I had wings, I would fly there immediately...." Xiao En became calm again. His intelligent daughter well understood her father's thoughts. Walking gingerly to the door, she opened it and she stuck her head out for a look around; the moonlight illuminated the vast black sky. Turning around, her eyes glowed fiercely in the dark, "To the Ding mansion...?"

"I'll kill each and every one of them!"

After wrapping his dagger in a coat, Guiying handed it to her father with trembling hands. She asked him timidly, "Father, are you really serious?"

Grasping the dagger in his hand, he stood up trembling and said, "You stay here and guard our home!" Without turning back, he strode out of the house. Guiying called to him in a gentle voice as he shut the wooden door.

"What is it?" Xiao En asked angrily.

"I want to go along with you."

"I'm going to kill people. What do you want to tag along for?"

"Although I don't know how to kill, I can stand by and boost your courage."

Xiao En couldn't decide how to respond. He looked carefully at his timid but heroic daughter and noticing that her eyes revealed a mixture of hesitation and passion, he felt sad. But, after thinking it over for a moment, he felt a surge of happiness and nodded his head: she was truly his beloved daughter.

"Do you really have the courage?"

Guiying bit her lower lip and nodded slowly.

"Good! Get dressed and bring your dagger along!" Xiao En said with curt finality. "Also, you'd better bring the 'Qingding Pearl'* along."

Clutching the dagger, which she had wrapped in a bundle of clothing, she came of the back room, and stepped out of the house with her father without saying a word.

Guiying paused abruptly and said, "Father, the door is not shut."

Xiao En looked back and sighed. This was the first time she had strolled onto the difficult path of life, like a young bird which has just flew out of the nest. How very weak she seemed!

"Don't worry about the door." Xiao En didn't want to mention the worst possible fate that might befall them on this trip, but hoped she would see his point. Much to his surprise, Guiying said, "How about all the furniture at home?" This made Xiao En somewhat annoyed.

_____

* The "Qingding Pearl" was Hua Rong's engagement present to Guiying. It was said that the pearl had the power to divide bodies of water, allowing one to cross rivers and lakes without getting wet. *The Qingding Pearl* is also used as a title for *The Fisherman's Revenge*.

"Let's just forget about this house and all the furniture as well!"

They walked to the river bank and boarded their boat and set sail. In the dark, Guiying made her way to the stern and found the rudder. Setting off from the dock, there was only darkness and silence, punctuated by the sound of the oars. As they proceeded down the river, their home gradually became nothing more than a vague shadow in the darkness.

Xiao En said, "Traveling in a boat in the night is different from traveling the day time. Make sure to maintain the direction!" As the little boat floated towards the center of the river, the two of them remained silent. Xiao En stared ahead into the darkness. On the opposite bank, he could see a number of dim lights. For many years, the fire in Xiao En's heart was nearly extinguished, but now it had burst into flame again. He imagined that this little flame could brighten the darkness, destroy the enemy's lair, and turn the opposite bank into a vast sea of scarlet fire.

"Father," Guiying's soft voice emerged from the stern. "I'm afraid. Do you really intend to kill them?"

"I told you not to come, but you insisted. Now we are almost half way there. If you want to change your mind!" Xiao En rowed harder in order to turn the boat around. He was having difficulty doing this, and realized that Guiying was working against him to keep the boat moving forward.

"I can't leave you!"

Hearing this heart-rending cry, Xiao En stopped rowing. Tears ran his old face.

Without warning, a tongue of flame flared up in the dark, quickly becoming a vast sea of flame.

The dialogue between father and daughter before entering the Ding mansion was like this:

"Have you got the 'Qingding Pearl'?"

"Yes, why do you ask?"

"If by any chance everything goes wrong, try to escape to the Hua's home by water!"

"How about you?"

"Don't worry about me, my child."

The Jade Bracelet

This is a frequently performed opera which is designed for the "huadan" (lively young girl) role. Simple in plot, it relies mainly on dramatic technique to entertain its audiences.

This ancient story of a young country girl's awakening to first love is brought to life on stage by the vivid gestures of the female protagonist: the delicacy of her motions as she does needlework, her graceful posture as she feeds the chickens and her shyness as she engages in flirtation with a young man and jests with the goodnatured old matchmaker.

The item "The Jade Bracelet" is the first part of the story featured in the opera "The Temple of Karmic Law."

— Ed. —

It was a sunny afternoon in spring. A gentle breeze stirred the branches of the weeping willow that stood by the door of the house. Fluttering leaves brushed across Sun Yujiao's brow, disturbing her thoughts. She was quite alone, for her mother had gone out, leaving her in the company of a handful of chickens that pecked for grain in the grass around her feet. But these creatures could hardly keep her amused with their cackling. She smiled, moved a chair outside and took up her sewing basket. Removing a pair of shoes, she examined the fine embroidery work that had yet to be completed. These were her own shoes, though by no means the only pair she had embroidered for herself. Yet she wondered if she would ever have an opportunity to wear such fine shoes. She selected a length of thread, matched it against her work, and then changed it for another. She smoothed out this second thread between her fingers, inserted it into her needle and began to sew. For a young girl of seventeen, there could be no more pleasant way to while away a spring afternoon. Indeed, she was soon quite absorbed in her work. Her thin, nimble fingers, as white as lily flowers, worked ceaselessly in a steady rhythm, like the hands of a lute player over the strings. Nevertheless, she remained constantly alert to all movements and activities taking place in the quiet, secluded street. How she hoped that someone would walk along that street — a child, an old man . . . anyone. Surely this street was there for people to walk along; if not, what other purpose could it serve? Of course, a street should be filled with people, but here passers-by were very few and far between.

That afternoon, however, a young man came strolling by. At first he appeared at the end of the street, but seeing that it was so long and deserted, he turned towards a more animated part of town. But some strange force seemed to attract him to that lonely spot, and he turned around once more and went back. In the distance, he could see a flock of hens under a willow tree and a young girl sewing with her head lowered to her work. He could only see her indistinctly, but he noticed that she had a head of thick, radiant black hair decorated with silver hairpins, a thoroughly lovely apparition. He hesitated, but as she chanced to raise her head, he saw her eyes, which made up his mind for him, and he slowly moved in her direction.

As he strolled forward, he thought of how he could strike up a conversation with this mysterious young girl. If only he could get her to stand up and speak to him, he would be able to hear her voice and observe her graceful figure. Perhaps she is shy, he thought, yet she seems so poised and natural....

So far, his plans met few snags. He went up to her and enquired about buying two roosters from the flock. She answered that she was unable to help him since her mother, who kept charge of the chickens, was not at home. Such was her simple reply, but behind these few words, a great deal was expressed. In their first brief encounter, they seemed to have discovered a wealth of knowledge about each other, to have shared their innermost secrets.

The young girl felt she should end this strange meeting since there were so few appropriate things to say. She picked up her chair and headed for the house, but discovered that the young man, whose name was Fu Peng, was blocking the door. He hurriedly stood aside to let her pass, and she shut the door carefully behind her. Sun Yujiao was unable to drop this incident from her mind, and began to wonder whether Fu Peng was still lingering outside. She opened the door again and to her surprise, encountered once again that same pair of dreamy eyes. Then she closed the door, leaving the young man standing alone.

Fu Peng's heart was moved by these meaningful exchanges, yet he felt he had to clarify his doubts. Young people in the pangs of first love are always full of resourcefulness; he took out one of a pair of jade bracelets given to him by his mother, placed it in front of the door, knocked once, and stole away. Should she pick it up and thus accept this token of love, then....

The young girl, still unable to tear her thoughts away from the strange young man, opened the door once more. But she was much more cautious this time. First she peeped out to make sure that nobody was around, and only then crept out nervously. As she stepped forward, her foot touched a hard object. She looked down and saw

the bracelet on the ground, realizing where it had come from and knowing all too well the message it implied. She was in an awkward plight now, for she knew that according to the rules of conduct proper to a young lady, she should harden her heart and return inside as if nothing had happened. But she was unable to bring herself to do this. Instead, she tried to muster up enough courage to pick up the bracelet. She knew that she could not let anyone guess the meaning of her action, and that she had to behave in a way that would provoke no comment. She called out, asking if anyone nearby had lost anything, but received no reply. She then took out a handkerchief she had tucked into her breast, and while shooing the chickens, deftly dropped it over the bracelet. Her heart

beat wildly and she rubbed her hands nervously as she carefully surveyed the quiet street, drawing the bracelet towards her with her foot as she did so. Finally she plucked up enough courage to bend down and nonchalantly pick up the bracelet and handkerchief together.

Quite unknown to her, however, two people were secretly watching her every action. One of them was Fu Peng himself. The moment he saw her snatch up the bracelet, he stepped up in front of her and cried out: "Young lady!"

"Take it away, take it away!" replied Sun Yujiao, desperately wishing that this incident had never occurred and that she had another pair of hands with which to return the bracelet to him. Who could tell if he was really sincere? Or if this was just a cunning trap?

"This is a present for you," he urged, finally clearing up her doubts.

"Take it away, I don't want it!" Her voice rose to a high pitch, but the sentiments behind what she said were quite different from before.

After Fu Peng left, the second hidden spectator, Matchmaker Liu, appeared. In those days, the job of the matchmaker was not highly regarded, for the methods used by matchmakers to "draw happy couples together" were often not entirely honorable, though this does not mean that all matchmakers were evil-hearted.

Matchmaker Liu had followed this little incident from start to finish. She wanted to hear the whole story from the young girl herself and pick up a few useful tips to help her in her job. However, prying "confidential secrets" out of a young girl in the throes of a first love is no easy matter. She would have to coax the answers out of her by picking up whatever she could and supplementing this with her own experience.

Of course, the young girl was unable to stand up to the persistent questioning of the old matchmaker and in the end told her the whole story. Matchmaker Liu then agreed to deliver a token of her affection to Fu Peng and in this way help them to cement their love. Perhaps it was Matchmaker Liu's sympathy for the newfound love of the two youths that stimulated her to perform this task for them.

The Temple of Karmic Law

In its entirety, this opera includes the episode "The Jade Bracelet" with Sun Yujiao as the protagonist. Because the present episode of the opera concerns a girl named Song Qiaojiao, the entire opera is also known by the name "The Fortuitous Encounter Between the Two Women Named Jiao." The story goes that after the handsome youth Fu Peng gave a jade bracelet to the country girl Sun Yujiao, he became implicated in a murder case. By coincidence, just at the time when the magistrate of Meiwu County erroneously found him guilty of murder, the empress dowager, accompanied by the eunuch Liu Jin, who was then at the height of his power, went to the Temple of Karmic Law to offer incense. There they encountered Song, who appealed to them to reverse the wrong verdict which had been imposed upon her fiance Fu Peng.

The chief protagonist of this episode of the opera is the county magistrate, who sings several long arias. This opera, like many other Peking Operas, was created cooperatively by the performers who were to play the leading roles, giving special consideration to the presentation of the singing and acting.

— Ed. —

Song Qiaojiao waited expectantly in front of the main entrance of the Temple of Karmic Law. When she first arrived, she hid behind one of the two large stone lions guarding the temple gates. Inside the temple not a single sound could be heard. Before long, a number of soldiers and eunuchs began arriving on horseback. After riding straight into the temple courtyard and leashing their horses to the trees, they began strutting about and ordering the monks to sweep the temple buildings and make ready a special chamber for the empress dowager's arrival. From where she stood, Song Qiaojiao could not observe the proceedings very clearly and, figuring she could not remain where she was for very long, decided to move to the shade of a scholartree, from where she could see the monks walking one by one out of the temple gate. They all had their own brooms, and busied themselves sweeping the road leading up to the temple and dispersing the crowd of curiosity seekers that had begun to gather. Contrary to custom, even the elder monks took part, and with eyebrows raised, directed the activities, shouting with their husky voices and huffing and puffing as they strutted about. It was apparent that something very unusual was about to happen. The rumors Song Qiaojiao heard turned out to be true: the empress dowager was on her way to the temple to offer her blessings.

Song Qiaojiao gnashed her teeth in anger as flames of rage rose within her. The Meiwu County magistrate had forced her into a corner, from which there was no apparent means of escape. Several weeks earlier, the magistrate contrived to have Song Qiaojiao's fiance Fu Peng thrown in jail without a single word of explanation. Fu Peng was accused of murder — a double murder in fact. Although they were not yet married, Song Qiaojiao knew Fu Peng as well as she knew herself: he was a typical pale-faced scholar who lacked courage to kill a chicken. Murder was totally out of the question. However, no one

154

should ever forget that the world is full of "responsible officials" who rely upon instruments of torture to perform their regular duties. Acting on the first bit of evidence which comes to light, these officials save themselves endless worry. Officials are all the same: in fact, anyone who becomes an official acquires the right to sit in a fancy office, gesticulate wildly and foam at the mouth with their eyes bulging with rage.

As Song Qiaojiao thought about this, her frustration became almost unbearable. She stared hard at the gate of the temple, but there was nothing there for her to see.

How had innocent Fu Peng become a victim in this affair? The whole story revolves around a jade bracelet. The befuddled county magistrate noticed Sun Yujiao wearing a particularly lovely jade bracelet one day, and soon learned that it had originally belonged to Fu Peng. Actually, Fu had dropped it by mistake in front of Sun Yujiao's house where the young woman had picked it up. Yet the question remained whether Fu had indeed lost it, or perhaps.... In any case, Sun Yujiao now had the bracelet in her possession, and was bold enough to wear it in public. Thinking about this set Song Qiaojiao off on another fit of teeth-gnashing. In all fairness, Fu Peng should have assumed responsibility for his own carelessness, quietly letting the issue drop. But was this something she could really let go of entirely?

By this time, the sunlight was beaming through the treetops, and in the distance Song Qiaojiao saw a large pale yellow sedan chair, surrounded by attendants beating drums, leading horses, and waving flags and giant fans. The personal attendants of the empress dowager held their ceremonial staffs directly in front of them and stared ahead as they walked, their faces entirely devoid of expression. This sight was somewhat terrifying to Song Qiaojiao. The sedan chair stopped in front of the temple and, led by the old monks, the entire population of the temple surged forward and kneeled down to greet the empress dowager. At this point, a particularly ferocious-looking official about 50 years of age dressed in a gold-embroidered robe stepped forward and lifted the curtain of the sedan chair. The strange thing was that his face was entirely hairless. Another attendant holding a horsehair duster approached from behind and took over holding the curtain. At this moment a splendidly dressed old woman stepped totteringly out of the sedan chair. Song Qiaojiao knew this was the empress dowager. This was her one-in-a-million chance to run up to the sedan chair and proclaim that an injustice had been committed, but she suddenly felt as if a large foreign object were caught in her throat. After several more minutes, she finally managed to stir up enough courage, and shouted, "An injustice has been committed," but by this time the empress dowager had already entered the temple and was sitting in a side hall drinking tea.

Song Qiaojiao began to have regrets about what she had just done. Since the temple was composed of a series of large courtyards, if the empress dowager were sitting in the central Mahavira Hall, would she have heard her cry? How much better it would have been if she had seized the chance to shout just as the empress was alighting from her sedan chair. But her musings were interrupted by an attendant armed with a sword, who strode out of the gates of the temple in search of the woman who had shouted aloud.

Gritting her teeth again, Song Qiaojiao stepped ˙ ward. In a gruff voice, the attendant said, "So it's you who had the audacity to shout aloud! Do you realize what you risk by frightening the empress?" Then he smiled, revealing a huge mouthful of white teeth. "If it weren't for Old Buddha's boundless mercy, you would have lost your head long ago." Song Qiaojiao removed her written petition from her robe and showed it to the attendant, who quickly turned on his heels and headed back into the temple.

Song Qiaojiao followed him through the temple gates and into the Mahavira Hall, where she kneeled down in reverence. From this position, she stole a glance into the main hall. The empress dowager was seated on a throne in the center of the hall. Seated next to her was the beardless eunuch whom she had noticed earlier, the famous Liu Jin, better known as "Nine Thousand Years".* Next to him stood the young eunuch Jia Gui, who had held up the curtain of the empress dowager's sedan chair.

Song Qiaojiao heard a very strange sound coming from outside the hall, a mixture of the roaring of tigers, the howling of wolves, and the whistling of a strong wind. The sound flooded into the hall like the crashing of ocean waves. This was actually the armed guards hailing the "tiger-like prowess" of Nine Thousand Years. The many stories Song Qiaojiao had heard about Liu Jin made her wonder just how much power this Nine Thousand Years wielded, since according to his title, he was only one thousand years "younger" than the emperor himself. As far as she knew, there was only one official known as Nine Thousand Years in the whole country, and whenever people mentioned his name, they would shiver with an

---

* Chinese emperors were addressed as "Ten Thousand Years".

undescribable terror and automatically lower their voices. Despite this, the common people had many stories to tell about him, although to Nine Thousand Years himself, the life of a common person was worth less than that of a chicken. Song Qiaojiao wondered if a man like Liu Jin was at all capable of dispensing justice, and whether or not he would act on her behalf. But when she rose to deliver her testimony, all of her fear and hesitation suddenly vanished. Barely glancing at her written petition, she presented all the details of the case one by one to the assembled audience.

Compared to Nine Thousand Years' voice, which was as brilliant as a clap of thunder, the empress dowager's voice sounded like the buzzing of mosquitos. The empress dowager rose from her seat and was herded away by a large bevy of attendants. With great ceremony, Nine Thousand Years sat down on her throne. After conferring briefly with Jia Gui, Nine Thousand Years raised his scepter and boomed forth: "Bring the county magistrate of Meiwu County before me!" Then immediately lowering his voice he said, "When that 'responsible official' of yours arrives, be sure to tell him the entire story. You may speak boldly; you have nothing to fear."

Song Qiaojiao felt like she was in a dream. Nine Thousand Years' rank was infinitely higher than the county magistrate's. A thorough appreciation of the Meiwu County magistrate's character led her to suppose that Nine Thousand Years would be an unendurable tyrant — at least as intimidating as the giant sculptures of the Four Heavenly Kings placed at the entrance to the temple. Thus it came as a great surprise that Nine

Thousand Years spoke to her in a kindly manner which helped her to bolster her self-confidence. This was all very difficult for her to understand. Song Qiaojiao felt that Nine Thousand Years was one of the nicest people she had ever met. Perhaps all the bad things people said about him weren't true after all. And it was also possible that making this visit to the temple in company with the empress dowager had a pacifying effect on his otherwise impetuous character.

When the Meiwu County magistrate finally appeared, he was made to kneel down next to Song Qiaojiao, which inspired in her an indescribable feeling of relief. In the past, whenever she had appeared before this magistrate, she was forced to kneel before him and prohibited from raising her head for even a glance: in other words, their respective positions were as far apart as heaven and hell. But in the presence of Nine Thousand Years, they suddenly became equals. One look at this thoroughly intimidated county magistrate shaking in his boots, Song Qiaojiao had to bite her lip to stop herself from laughing out loud.

Nine Thousand Years came right to the point. "In regard to the alleged stabbing which took place at night in front of the Sun Village resulting in the death of two persons: Firstly, there is no weapon to serve as evidence; secondly, there are no witnesses to the event; and Fu Peng, a hereditary commander of the armed forces, has been imprisoned." The county magistrate retorted that he had obtained Fu Peng's confession, to which Nine Thousand Years replied, "But it was you who bought him the knife." Jia Gui handed a written petition to the county magistrate and said, "During his appointment as a 'responsible official', having failed to perform any good deeds on behalf of those citizens under his charge, he has been removed from his office through the action of a petition drafted by his constituents." When the county magistrate read the signature on this petition, he hesitated long enough for Song Qiaojiao to say to him, "Your honor! How could you ever forget your favorite little maiden?" And with that, Song Qiaojiao laughed revengefully and relieved herself of the great burden of anxiety which had long laid heavily on her heart.

It was determined that the verdict would be handed down by Nine Thousand Years three days hence.

In the interim, the county magistrate was ordered to round up all the persons involved in the crime and to investigate the facts of the case. Song Qiaojiao went home to await the final disposition. But before she left, Nine Thousand Years handed her a gift of one ingot of silver and said, "You appear to be the victor in this case, although the final decision remains to be made. Take this small reward home with you and await our notification." As she left the great hall, she exchanged a few parting remarks with the county magistrate, whose authority was now deflated to a significant degree.

"Hey! Your honor. Look up there!" She pointed to the throne.

"What's up there?"

"A place where people actually respect the law."

"Your petition was truly a cunning piece of work. Are you not satisfied yet?"

"Ah! So now you know what your favorite little maiden's capable of!"

Song Qiaojiao slept poorly for the next few nights, and her dreams were interspersed with nightmares. At times she was hopeful, but she also worried about what

Nine Thousand Years held in store for her. In the end she clung to the hope that justice would prevail. Murderers paid for their crimes with their lives; the innocent would be set free. And corrupt officials like the county magistrate would receive their just punishment. Beyond this, there was very little she could be sure of.

The case was concluded with the murderers and the instigators of the crime being brought swiftly to justice. Fu Peng was perfunctorily reprimanded and released from jail. But what came as a great surprise was that rather than being punished, the county magistrate was promoted to a higher official position. The only explanation Song Qiaojiao could come up with was that he had bribed Jia Gui. But even stranger than this was the arrangement Nine Thousand Years made for Sun Yujiao and Song Qiaojiao. "The loss of the jade bracelet was a mere blunder on the part of young Fu Peng. Song Qiaojiao deserves to be praised as a woman among women. Thus I give my personal decree that Song Qiaojiao, Sun Yujiao, and Fu Peng should make the most of this joyous occasion and be married three-in-one."

Song Qiaojiao could hardly believe her ears! Nine Thousand Years sat laughing heartily on his throne, as if his unexpected decision was the source of the greatest happiness for all parties concerned.

Song Qiaojiao and Sun Yujiao were escorted away and provided with lavish costumes for the wedding. Fu Peng donned an embroidered robe and stuck two golden flowers in his hat. Dressed in all her finery, Sun Yujiao smiled somewhat sheepishly at Song Qiaojiao, but the latter only turned her head the other way. In doing this, however, her eyes fell upon a broadly smiling Fu Peng, with his two golden flowers quivering gently above his head.

The Meiwu County magistrate's only "punishment" was to transmit an official document to the provincial administration office of Shaanxi Province, and see to it that a sum of 3,000 taels of silver be removed from the treasury and sent to Suzhou and Hangzhou to purchase wedding trousseaus for the two brides. This was all personally arranged by Nine Thousand Years. And after completing this mission, the Meiwu County magistrate was promoted and given a new official's hat.

The Two Strange Encounters

This opera, which is also known as "The Horse Trader's Chronicle", is an item traditionally included in the repertoire of Kunqu Opera, Peking Opera, Hanju (Hubei Opera) and Huiju (Anhui Opera).

The story goes that one day a man named Li Qi went out to trade horses, and upon his return he discovered that his son and daughter by his first wife had disappeared. Li thereupon inquired of his serving girl as to their whereabouts, and the girl, knowing that it was his second wife who had forced them to flee but not daring to tell the truth, committed suicide. Li's second wife then falsely accused him of raping and slaying the servant, and he was arrested by the magistrate of Baocheng County and put on death row. Li Qi's daughter, in the midst of flight, married a young man named Zhao Chong, who later passed the imperial examinations and was appointed the new magistrate of Baocheng County. Li Qi's son also passed the imperial examinations and was appointed inspector general, making him responsible for investigating all local criminal cases. The story below recounts how Li Qi's daughter, with the help of her husband, saved her father's life during a coincidental reunion with her brother.

— Ed. —

Zhao Chong, magistrate of Baocheng County, had just returned from an inspection trip in the countryside. Dismounting before the gate of his official residence, he dusted his clothes and shoes with his long sleeves and walked straight to his private quarters, calling again and again: "Get me some tea; I'm thirsty!" and "Hurry up with supper!"

As he downed the hot tea in mouthfuls, he kept looking around. "Where's Madame?" Even on an ordinary day, when he had finished work and returned to his private quarters, his newly wed wife would be waiting at the door of the back hall to remove his official cap and gown and ask after his health. How was it that having just returned from a long trip she should not be there to greet him? He had been away for a full week, during which time his thoughts of home had never left him. Did Guizhi not know this? On horseback and in his dreams, he had called her name a thousand times.

The young couple sat face to face in their chamber. On the table were some cups and saucers and a lamp with a red silk shade that gave off a warm glow. Guizhi was silent. When Zhao Chong raised his cup, she raised hers but merely touched it to her lips and set it down again.

"Are you sick?" he asked. She only shook her head quietly.

When Zhao Chong was away in the country, Guizhi had sat alone under the lamp at night working at her embroidery, often until very late. The rear of their house was separated from the county jail by only a high wall, and after nightfall the place was as silent as a graveyard. For several nights in succession, Guizhi had heard faint moans coming from the other side of the wall, sounds that were often piteous, apparently coming from an old man. It was so sorrowful that the young wife could not sleep; when she lay down, her eyes refused to close. She managed to put up with this for a few days, but then felt she could no longer wait. The night before, accompanied by her maid, she had ordered to have the jail doors opened and went inside to find out who it was. What she discovered was a terrible shock — the prisoner moaning

so piteously in the night was her own father, Li Qi! Between sobs, he told her how he had been framed by his second wife and given the death penalty. He was now awaiting execution.

How was she to tell her husband all this? Would he forgive her for being so bold as to enter the jail without his permission? How would he react if he knew that his father-in-law was a prisoner in the death row of his own jail?

In the dim lamplight, Zhao Chong held Guizhi's face close to his. He looked tenderly into her eyes wet with tears and gently smoothed her tightly knitted brows. She broke away and turned her head as if in anger, but could not escape her husband's caresses. As the tears rolled down, she managed to smile wryly.

Zhao Chong learned that this was an unjust case left over from the last magistrate. The decision had been approved by a higher court and the prisoner was to be executed in the fall. As a paternal official, it was his duty to protect the people and defend the law. As a son-in-law, he could not see his own relative unjustly put to death. And as a husband, he did not have the heart to see his beloved wife in such an abject state of sorrow and despair. He knew that if he failed to right this wrong, his own life would be ruined and his chambers would be full of only sobs and tears instead of smiles and laughter. Whether he admitted it or not, this was a great threat and a misfortune he must by all means try to prevent.

But he was only a newly appointed magistrate, a minor official. He had no power to reverse the verdict of a case that had already been decided; his duty was to carry out orders.

Zhao Chong was unwilling to reveal these problems to his wife. He would rather give her a glimmer of hope, no matter how illusory, if it would only lift the clouds from her brows.

"I have a way," he said, raising his brows. "I read an urgent message yesterday. It said that the new provincial judge was on an inspection tour and would stop at Baocheng. I've been told that this is a new *jinshi*,* a young and clever man, not one of those old muddleheads. If the case could be retried by him, there was hope for overturning the verdict and redressing the wrong."

"Then all we have to do is submit a plaint to His Excellency...?" asked Guizhi.

"Yes, but first we must write it and submit it to His Excellency in person. The person doing this must be a relative of the prisoner and one who will answer for his action in court."

Guizhi's brows knitted again. "And the plaint?" she murmured.

"I can write that."

"You know how?"

"It should be easy for a county magistrate, a dignitary of the seventh rank who tries civil cases day after day."

"If we have the plaint, then everything will be all right. I'll hand it in myself even if it costs me my life."

"Do you really think you can do it?" asked Zhao Chong with a surge of inexplicable pity and regret. The girl's naivety had touched him deeply. "Have you ever witnessed the pomp and dignity of a provincial judge on a

---

* *Jinshi*—one who has passed the highest level of imperial examination.

tour? With his long train of officials, guards and attendants, you'd be trampled under feet by the horses before
you even saw his face."

The two worked on composing the plaint until it was
past midnight, and were up again in the wee hours of the
morning after hardly a wink of sleep.

Long before daybreak, Zhao Chong donned his red
official robes and hurried off to the county house where
preparations for the provincial judge's arrival were being

made. It was only after everything was in order that he returned home for breakfast. By this time, Guizhi had dressed up as a magistrate's page in plain clothes and black cap, according to the plans they had made the night before. The disguise could hoodwink a casual observer, but her headful of thick black hair made her cap stand too high, showing her pretty white face, which was a little too delicate for an official's personal attendant anyway.

Zhao Chong told her to take a few steps. They did not look like the strides of an official's attendant; in fact, they did not even look like a man's.

So now he had to teach her how to walk in a man's boots, letting her arms dangle freely at her sides instead of placing them before her chest, and how to look solemn with no trace of shyness or anxiety. He also showed her how to conceal the plaint in her garments. After the judge had received the last of his subordinates, he would be ready to leave the hall. At that point, she was to make a loud cry, take a step forward, fall on her knees before the steps of the hall and hold the plaint above her head until a bailiff took it from her.

Guizhi listened attentively, nodding from time to time and fixing in her mind everything he said. She saw her husband suppress his anxiety and force a smile, and felt such deep gratitude in her heart that she forgot his repeated exhortations to not cry and began sobbing. Throwing herself into his arms, she buried her face in his bosom and let out a flood of tears that wetted the embroidered insignia on the chest of his new red robes.

The provincial judge's temporary headquarters bustled with activity like a country fair. Outside the front entrance was a row of placards inscribed "Silence" and "Keep away" or bearing some long official title. Pairs of huge red silk lanterns with the words "Inspecting Commissioner" were hung all about. Horses were tethered under the willows on a large square to the east, while crowds of onlookers formed a human wall in the distance. Local officials here to pay their respects to the judge dismounted from their horses or stepped out of their sedan chairs in front of the entrance and walked in. After presenting their documents, they came out again and lined up along the two sides of the courtyard. Zhao Chong and Guizhi had entered the compound ahead of the others. He motioned to the girl to hide beside the second gate, and went in to present himself to his superior in the main hall. He then came out and stood beside the gate to hear the judge's address.

When the ceremony was over, all officials high and low filed out of the second gate in order of rank, but Zhao Chong was privileged to remain there until the very last. Seeing that the courtyard before the main hall was nearly empty, he turned and glanced behind him. Everything was proceeding according to plan. Crying "He's innocent!" a page in plain clothes and black cap stepped forward and fell upon his knees beside the paved path, holding a piece of paper above his head that continually flapped in the wind.

The judge seated in the hall asked a few questions, which were answered by the bailiffs. Then one of them came down and took the plaint. The page was summoned into the hall and, though Zhao Chong could not hear clearly what they were saying, he concluded that it was only a routine questioning. But suddenly there was a profound silence and there seemed to be no further developments. How slowly the minutes crept by! Zhao Chong was like an ant on a hot frying pan, but he dared not go in to see what was going on. He began to regret having conceived this plan. The judge must have seen through Guizhi's disguise, which would suffice to have her arrested and tried. Thinking of Guizhi in custody, he did not know what to do. Had he not been in the judge's headquarters, he would have torn his hair in agony and called out aloud to heaven and earth.

Things certainly looked bad. He heard the bailiffs shout, "Close the gates!" and in an instant the great hall was empty. An old man walked slowly over to close the second gate and was surprised to find Zhao Chong still standing there.

"Are you still waiting? His Excellency has left the hall. He won't be back today."

Zhao Chong stared hard at the old man and strode over to the hall. Sure enough, the judge, his seconds, secretaries and attendants — were all gone, including Guizhi. There only remained a young janitor sweeping the floor.

"Did you see that girl who submitted the plaint just then? No, no, I mean the plaintiff. Where, where is he now?"

The janitor stopped sweeping and looked amusingly at this county magistrate who seemed to have gone out of his mind. "Oh, that plaintiff? His Excellency read the plaint, saw that she was a woman in disguise, and had her taken to the rear hall for questioning." Then, as a mischievous smile played about his face, he lowered his voice and asked, "What is she to you?"

"Bastard!" snarled the magistrate, who turned and rushed to the rear hall, but suddenly stopped in his tracks.

Having caused a disturbance in the judge's head-quarters, Zhao Chong was taken into the rear hall and now stood quaking before His Excellency. He could not answer the janitor's question just then; still less could he do it here.

"Who is that plaintiff?"

"He's your humble servant's..." answered Zhao Chong, his face turning purple.

Zhao Chong was boiling with anger. He hated himself for his stupidity and hated the judge for being so harsh in his ways. Then he cursed himself for his cowardice, for being like a mouse in the claws of a cat, daring not to speak the truth and acknowledge his own

wife. Gritting his teeth, he threw off his black gauze cap, fell on his knees and cried out: "That plaintiff is my wife. . . ." He raised his head and saw a playful smile on the judge's face, at which he cursed himself again: "The heartless wretch!" At that moment the richly dressed Guizhi swaggered out from behind a screen, her face also wreathed in smiles. Zhao Chong was confounded. He forgot what he wanted to say and only stared with his mouth wide open and his eyes burning as if they would consume somebody.

Guizhi walked slowly to the back of the judge's desk, placed a delicate hand on his right shoulder and whispered something in his ear. Then both turned and smiled at Zhao Chong.

The short spell of silence went on for an age.

No wonder it all seemed like a dream to Zhao Chong. Guizhi and the judge, too, were greatly surprised. In the extraordinary circumstances of that morning, Guizhi had found a long lost brother, Zhao Chong had paid his respects to both his superior and his brother-in-law, and Li Qi, the old convict in the death cell, had become a venerable father and a dignitary by paternal rights. It was not surprising that when he was brought before his son, daughter and son-in-law, he kept wondering if it weren't a dream. He looked closely at Guizhi, a daughter who had been sent away by her family, as if he were not sure. Guizhi straightened her robes, took a few steps forward and said to her father, "Your daughter is a lady now!" She tried to control her feelings, but teardrops welled up in the corners of her eyes.

The Affinity of the Iron Bow

The following story is an episode from the opera "The Legends of Distinguished Heroes." The plot is based on the will which a man gives to his daughter, a young tea peddler: that only the man who can bend his iron bow can have her hand in marriage.

The story recounts how a strong, handsome young scholar goes to a teahouse where he sees a local despot taking liberties with the young girl. A struggle ensues between them, and the scholar manages to drive the bully off. Then he succeeds in bending the iron bow, demonstrating that he is qualified to marry the girl. Later, after undergoing much difficulty, they once again defeat the bully, who is now bent on revenge, and are finally happily united in marriage.

The actress Guan Shushuang, who excels at playing many different roles in Peking Opera, made a great sensation when she performed in this opera both in China and in Europe.

— Ed. —

Along both sides of the highway, about a mile from town, stood rows of one-story houses — inns, smithies, fruitstalls, and groceries. In front of the wineshop hung the customary cloth sign; in the meat shop the butcher, naked to the waist, stood behind the counter boning meat.

175

This was a marketplace of about a hundred households conveniently situated close to town on the road to the Dongyue Temple. On the 1st and 15th of each month, when fairs were held at the temple, there was a thriving trade, for most passers-by would stop here for a drink or rest.

On this day of incense-burning, the sun had just peeped over the horizon when the first customers arrived at the shop doors. The morning trade began two hours earlier than usual.

At one end of the marketplace was a two-room house with a thatched roof and freshly whitewashed walls. A matshed erected in front of the house gave the small courtyard a cool and quiet appearance; inside the house, it was fairly dark. At one corner of the matshed hung a blue cloth sign with the three words "Home of Heroes", a name somewhat inappropriate for a small teashop. Four or five white wooden tables were placed randomly inside the shed. Two of the rooms at the back, however, was neatly furnished; this, no doubt, was for special guests. In hot weather, most people preferred to have their tea in the shed, from where they could watch the flow of traffic on the road and the goings-on in the neighborhood.

The small teashop was staffed by a woman and her daughter. At this moment the mother, a woman in her fifties, was sitting on a chair by the roadside, fanning herself as she carried on a desultory conversation with her daughter who was clearing away the pots and cups left by customers. Somehow the two got into an argument.

"Mother, this is awful. These vagrants who come here every day are such a nuisance. They don't come for tea. They're...."

She broke off and sullenly continued clearing away the tea cups, sweeping the floor and rearranging the tables and chairs. Her mother did not answer; she merely glanced at her daughter with a thin smile. In her heart she knew why the little teashop was becoming noisier day by day. She knew, too, that her daughter was growing up and would judge and react to things on her own; she had experienced this herself. Still, she could not quite fathom what was on her daughter's mind. Her eyes were fixed on her daughter: on her shirt and trousers of blue cloth, on her light blue apron with the lovely embroidered designs along the edges, and on her jet black hair done up in two buns, with a large red pomegranate flower at one temple. It was by imitating this pomegranate flower that she embroidered the flowers on her apron.

"Mother, why aren't you talking?" she asked, betraying her displeasure and willfulness. "I never want to serve those vagabonds again. You can tell from the roguish look in their eyes they're not decent people. Next time we have customers like them, you better take care of them. . . ." She looked at her mother, who remained silent.

"My dear child, we are running a teashop. We can't choose our customers, letting in some and refusing others." The old woman's reasoning could hardly be rebutted. "But your mother knows who's good and who's bad. Didn't I kick out the gang that was just here?"

She was referring to a gang of rascals with a "lord" in their midst who had sneered, fussed, insulted and pounded the tables and stools a few hours before. Sensing the danger, she had sent her daughter away and waited on them herself. It was fortunate that the girl was not there; had she been present and heard everything, a brawl might have ensued.

"Mother knows," continued the woman, speaking more calmly. "I'll take care of the teashop. If any unwelcome guest comes in, you just stay away. I can handle them.... Why did we open this shop in the first place? Wasn't it because of that bow your father left us? When a strongman who can bend that bow comes here and takes it away, your mother's heart will rest at ease." Her voice was getting softer and slower all the time, as if she were talking in her sleep. She was, after all, an old woman, and more and more talkative every year. For some reason, she was always thinking of the bow, though the very mention of it would silenced her daughter, who would stop pestering her mother and run away.

The girl entered the room for special guests in the back. No guests had been in there that day so there was no need to tidy up. She walked over to the back wall. In the center of its whitewashed surface hung a somewhat faded landscape painting that showed a man on horseback, a bow slung over his shoulder and a sword at his side, galloping away in the hills. She often meditated on the painting, but could not guess where the rider was going or when he would arrive. Hanging to the right of the painting was a polished brightly jet black bow. Its grip was well worn and the core was showing in several places; but it was still a fine carved bow, with a stave of iron and core of bronze, ancient and exceedingly rare. Weapons like this had not been seen in tournaments and war games for generations, the reason being that no one nowadays was strong enough to bend them. She reached over and took down the bow, pulled out a handkerchief and began to polish it gently. There was no dust on it; the string was new. A slight scent could be detected on the stave, for the girl was in the habit of taking down the bow and drawing it a number of times every day.

"Come out, girl, and make some tea," shouted her mother.

She had returned to her room, where she waited until her mother had called several times before answering in a lazy drawl. She took from the stove the earthen pot for boiling water, casually picked up a stack of coarse blue-and-white cups and walked out. When she entered the guest room, she noticed a new customer sitting at the table looking outside. She could only see two ribbons hanging from the back of his headdress, but these told her that he was a scholar. Hesitating for an instant, she withdrew.

From behind the door she listened to their conversation. It was clear from the woman's tone of voice that she liked the young man, for it was not the way she customarily spoke to clients, with a noticeable trace of impatience. Mother was in good humor, and the young man answered her softly and civilly. The conversation flitted from subject to subject; then somehow the young man noticed the bow on the wall and asked about it. The old woman brightened up at this and with great enthusiasm told him the origin, history and nature of the bow. It was left to her by her deceased husband, she said, "He could bend the bow, but when he died, not a single man in the entire district who could do it."

The girl had heard this story repeatedly, but of late her mother seemed more eager than before to tell it. She would often interrupt her mother in the midst of the story, yet strange to say it always sounded very new to her. This was because of a secret shared by the two of them. She was worried now lest her mother should unwittingly let the secret become known and wanted to interrupt her, but she felt rooted to the floor and could not move a step. Suddenly she heard a buzzing in her ears that drowned out her mother's voice. It was usual for the old woman to wind up her story by saying, "The master of this house said that as long as he was alive, he could bend the bow, but after his death, his little daughter would be the only one capable of doing it. If there is another man in this town who can bend the bow, he shall be our son-in-law." She imagined her mother saying all this, though their conversation was quite inaudible; but how could she tell it all to a total stranger?

She placed the teapot and cups before the scholar, but forgot to pour out tea, forgot everything in fact, as the two looked each other over. Her mother was not at all vexed upon seeing this; she poured the tea herself. Noticing her mother grinning, the girl turned and ran away.

She was called out again, and this time her mother told her that the young man wanted to see her bend the bow three times, after which he would do it three times himself.

Archery was second nature to the girl; not a day passed without her practicing it in the backyard. And when she practiced, she bent the bow countless times in a great variety of positions. She could draw the bow to the full, then with feet planted firmly lower her body until it almost touched the ground, and in this position release an arrow. According to legend, this was the position assumed by Hou Yi of the Xia dynasty when he shot down nine suns and saved the crops on earth from being scorched. She did not believe that anybody could shoot an arrow at the sun, nor could she imagine how powerful a bow would be needed still, she loved the story and felt that she ought to be able to hit any target she aimed at.

Though there were only two spectators, she felt as if she were standing in a huge arena with thousands looking on. The bow, when she took it down, seemed to be heavier than usual. She assumed the proper stance and took aim, but she was constantly aware of the eyes that were watching her. She went through the various movements perfunctorily, drawing the string back till the bow was round and then releasing it three times. Yet she was very dissatisfied with her performance. She could hear her own

breathing and the pounding of her heart, something that had never occurred during her daily practice. Flinging down the bow, she threw herself into her mother's arms. "Mother, what's happening?" she asked softly. "My heart's beating so fast."

The scholar now picked up the bow, stood at the same spot and bent the bow three times. She buried her face in her mother's bosom, peeping out with one eye, then pointing and gesturing, she whispered in her mother's ear: "We pluck the string with only two fingers; he grabs it with the whole hand. That's incorrect, mother."

"Each master archer has his own way. Your method is correct, but so is his," she answered with a smile as she fondled her daughter's burning cheeks.

The girl looked up at her mother's face and noticed a faint smile among her wrinkles. Her gray hair was fluttering slightly in the breeze, and the girl reached up and gently smoothed it with her hand. There were many questions she wanted to ask, but she lacked the courage. She was thinking about the conversation between her mother and the young scholar; what a pity she didn't catch the second and most important part! Did her mother reveal everything? It seemed that her mother could read her thoughts, but she only smiled.

A Startling Dream of Wandering Through the Garden

"A Startling Dream of Wandering Through the Garden" is an episode in the opera "The Peony Pavilion", one of the four plays authored by the celebrated Chinese dramatist Tang Xianzu (1550-1616) which take dreams as their theme. It is a standard item in the repertoire of Kunqu Opera and is also performed in Peking Opera and other forms of traditional Chinese opera.

Peking Opera is a theatrical form based on a combination of Huiju (Anhui Opera), Hanju (Hubei Opera), Qinqiang (Shaanxi Opera) and Kunqu Opera. However, in Peking Opera there are a number of items which are sung in the pure Kunqu style, and "A Startling Dream" is one of them.

The story in this episode goes that the female protagonist had a dream in which she saw a handsome youth, and upon waking up, in the excess of her disappointment, became fatally ill and was buried in a garden after her death. Later, this youth, now a high official, encountered the ghost of the female protagonist in the garden, causing her to come back to life. Subsequently she married the youth and they became a distinguished couple, bringing the play to a happy conclusion.

— Ed. —

The fine spring weather one afternoon was warm and muggy enough to cause the newly opened flowers to languish, the willow branches to droop, and the catkins to drift aimlessly.

Du Liniang could hardly hold her embroidery frame steady. She had stopped using her needle and was even finding it difficult to pull the colored thread; besides, it was so long. Heaving a sigh, she put her needle-work down.

Where was the maid Chunxiang now? Hiding in the back of the house, perhaps, and taking a nap.

Of late, she had a vague feeling that her mother was showing increased concern for her. Gently stroking her daughter's soft and thick black hair, the old lady would sigh as if there were many things on her mind. "My child, do you realize how hard it is to be a mother?" She looked up in wonder; though mother did not look after her personally, she knew that mother's thoughts were always with her. Indeed, it was hard to be a mother.

Mother had told her once: "A girl should not sleep during the day. Only lazy women do that. It shows a lack of discipline and education."

She had also said: "There's nobody in the garden, so young girls should keep out of it as much as possible. If by chance you should come across a flower demon or a tree monster, you never know what might happen."

Mother instructed her in many other ways. She loved her daughter and never scolded her, but her glance was very severe. What was permissible and what was not was readily discernible from those eyes, which could even define the range of her daughter's activities.

Du Liniang's chamber was provided with both a dressing table and a girl's toilet articles and an inkslab, brushes and paper. She liked to paint. In the beginning, she merely traced out flower designs; later, however, she also tried her hand at figure painting. She owned an album of women's portraits and in her leisure moments made copies from them. In her eyes, these ladies were very much like herself, all so beautiful and so elegant. And it seemed to her that they all had something on their minds. As she thought she had nothing on her mind, this was something rather odd to her, something she did not understand.

Besides this album of portraits, she also owned a book of biographies of women given her by her mother. The book contained many fine woodcuts of women accompanied by a story, usually a sad one. It seemed that women's misfortunes were always tied up with men. This, she thought, might be the reason why her mother had cautioned her so often. If she could only keep away from men all her life, perhaps she could also keep out of harm's way.

Indeed, besides her father and the old master in the study, Du Liniang had little opportunity to see other men. In her mind, the men in the world outside were different from those two, for how could people like them bring so much suffering to women?

Biographies of Famous Women told only of unfortunate women. There must be many stories of women who were more fortunate, but this author did not, or would not, write about them. So when her father was not at home, she would go secretly into his study and read the books there. Father had many books stacked on the shelves and numerous pamphlets and thin volumes of lesser note strewn about his desk and bed. She had to snatch at opportunities to read; whenever anyone came along, she would quickly put whatever book she was reading down. In this way she read many of the famous pieces in *Gems of Chinese Poetry*. Though there were no stories here, she could grasp the most intimate thoughts of the young heroes and heroines, which was as good as knowing the story. What surprised her more was that there should be a story as true-to-life and audacious as *The Love Story of Yingying*. It took her two sittings to finish this book. She meditated deeply as she read, her cheeks warming and her heart beating quickly, but she could not bear to read through to the end at one go....

Sitting in her boudoir on a warm spring afternoon, Du Liniang suddenly recalled the stories she had read. She not only remembered the details but could recite from memory the most striking passages. It was impossible for her to put them out of her mind even if she tried.

Chunxiang came in to help her dress and make up, after which they would go into the garden. "All the flowers are in bloom," said Chunxiang, "except the peony; and by the time it blooms spring will be over."

She sat down quietly before the mirror on the dressing table to have a look at herself. Seeing the blush on her cheeks and the languid look in her eyes, she turned her head to one side. The profile of a lovely girl appeared in the mirror, wearing a high bun and with a tiny ornament over her forehead that was still quivering. She was struck by her own beauty.

"My lady, you look wonderful today," remarked Chunxiang, "and this dress is perfect for you. Your bright orange blouse highlights your snow-white skin and jet black hair beautifully."

Du Liniang cast a quiet glance at her maid but said nothing.

With Chunxiang supporting her arm, she walked slowly out of her boudoir, cautiously trod over a moss-covered path and pushed open the garden door. A flood of light greeted her. Such a riot of colors, such blooming vitality, such brilliant sunshine too dazzling for the eyes—all had been shut out by just one small door!

She paused there, a bit dazed and confused, not knowing how to enter into that world of glorious sunlight. She recalled a line she had read somewhere: "Spring is as deep as the sea." Yes, indeed! Here was spring in its full glory, deep and mysterious like the sea.

Spring is not a time of placidity and stillness. Swallows dragging their forked tails brushed past them; orioles alighted on the highest branches of the willow. Singing or chirping, they too had been animated by the return of spring and were enjoying themselves. All nature was astir. The very flowers and grass were alive and had feelings, and knew what was gladness and sorrow; they knew that buds opened only to fade, that spring was beautiful but brief, and that such golden hours should not be allowed to slip by. But there were people who let such beauty slip by without so much as a glance. Today, if she had not risked offending her mother by coming secretly into the garden, all that she had just seen would have been as good as nothing.

She was deeply troubled; there were many things she wanted to say but knew not how to say, and there was no one present who could understand her feelings. Supported by Chunxiang, she walked past the gallery, flower beds and rockery, and came to a terrace beside a pavilion that stood on the bank of a pond. The hill beyond was ablaze with azaleas. In her distress, she wanted to be alone, so she sent Chunxiang away to see

whether her mother had awakened from her nap. Then sitting down on a stone bench and leaning against a boulder, she fell into a dreamy muse, her eyes fixed upon the pond and the bright aquatic flowers.

With Chunxiang gone, she regained her composure. Strange to say, the fearful loneliness she had felt a moment ago quickly dissipated. The spring breezes, the willows and poplars, the swallows and orioles, the fiery azaleas, the varicolored peonies, the lush green grass... everything before her had turned into conscious, emotional beings capable of transmitting their feelings and pouring out their grief. She remembered what her mother had said about flower demons. Sure enough, before her stood swarms of these endearing little creatures, demons or not. She leaned over the railing and looked down: there among the goldfish was her reflection. She was both surprised and gladdened to see it. She was not afraid of anybody eavesdropping, for she had no secrets worth keeping here; she would interrogate that foolish maiden hiding under water, and make her answer all the secret questions buried in her bosom, questions that could not be aired before her mother or Chunxiang.

She raised her head and saw emerging from among the rocks in the distance the figure of a youth in a white silk shirt, holding some green willow twigs. She looked at him carefully. His face was familiar, but she could not remember where she had seen it. She recalled at this instant the many references to breaking willow twigs she had read in ancient poems. Why was it that people always broke willow or poplar twigs when they parted with their loved ones or thought of friends far away?

The scholar with the twigs was smiling and slowly walking towards her. She sat there quietly, her heart perfectly calm; what she was expecting had come at last.

The scholar came up and sat down beside her. She could feel the rim of his hat touching the corner of her hair; she felt his breath upon her cheek; and she heard him whispering in her ear. It was inaudible, but what did that matter; they were words she had repeated to herself many times before.

At his suggestion, they got up and walked slowly, shoulder to shoulder, towards the garden. She did not speak, only listened; never, she felt, had her steps been so light and her heart so full. They walked beside the pond, watching the ducks swimming leisurely, and she suddenly remembered the line: "To be in a boat in springtime is like being seated in heaven." It was a wonderful line and she felt at this moment that she was in heaven too.

Tired from walking and talking, they chose a place among the rocks and sat down beneath a peach tree in bloom. They sat there for a long time, as the wind sent down showers of pink rain. Petals were strewn all over their heads and faces, but they sat without moving. Before long they would be buried beneath the pink shower....

The Four Successful Candidates

The triennial competitive examinations held over the course of more than one thousand years of Chinese history were the principal means of filling the ranks of the official bureaucracy. Success in these examinations brought instant fame to the winning candidates and a rapid rise in their position on the social scale. In addition, men whose names appeared together on the list of successful candidates for the same year shared a fraternity similar to that of alumni of the same university.

The present opera tells the story of four such officials and their different responses to a single lawsuit, thus exposing the official corruption and social inequality which was so much a part of life in old China.

— Ed. —

In the law court, Song Shijie was put in the cangue. As he was led out the main door, there were butterflies in his stomach; his hands were trembling and his legs wobbled as if he were walking on bales of cotton. Outside the gate of the government office, the sun was shining brightly. He paused and uttered a long sigh: "So I won in the end!" But what kind of victory was this?

The judge Mao Peng had said to Song Shijie: "There is a saying: 'Common people should never try to take officials to court.' But in one fell swoop you have lodged complaints against two high officials of the central government and one district magistrate. How can you possibly be innocent?"

Since Song Shijie himself had once been one of those "old gentlemen responsible for conducting lawsuits", he naturally understood the laws of the land. And although he was convicted on unusual grounds, there was nothing he could say, and he had to place all of his hopes on the arrival of a "just judge". He did actually receive kindness beyond the limits of the law: in consideration of his age, Song Shijie was exiled to the border regions to serve in the army. He was very satisfied, even to the extent of regarding Mao Peng with esteem and gratitude. But these were only transient emotions, and he soon discovered a harsh reality staring him in the face. He was old and frail, with neither daughters nor sons, and had been assigned alone to the distant borderland.... The thought of this was frightening. He had an aged wife and a home, and had lived a comfortable life. But suddenly a whirlwind had arisen under his feet sweeping everything away. It seemed like a dream.

But it was Song Shijie himself who had stirred up the whirlwind....

A young woman rushed towards him and threw herself sobbing at his feet: "Father! Father!" Song Shijie rubbed his old eyes. Was this person really his daughter? A young man stood next to her calling "Step-father!" What was this all about?

In the past, Song Shijie had led a leisurely and carefree life as a clerk in the criminal department. After leaving the *yamen* where he had worked for many years, Song opened a tiny inn outside the West Gate. With this small business, he would never have to become a jobless vagrant. His wife chided him everyday to "drink more wine and pay less attention to other people's affairs" in order to ensure that their remaining days would be spent in peace. He enjoyed both his wine and minding other people's business, and if he couldn't do both he'd become terribly itchy. But how great was his capacity? He had lost his official post because he "defied his superiors in carrying out his work", that is, his methods often clashed with those of his superiors; this could not be tolerated, it was too dangerous. Under his wife's supervision, when he had come across unpleasant incidents, he stood aside and watched, and then went home to tell her about it. No longer did he seek this kind of praise: "Well, old man, you'll learn someday to do as you're told. Next time you come up against this kind of thing, you'd better steer clear of it. Can you handle so many things at once?" Song Shijie nodded: "Do sweep the snow from your own doorstep, but don't bother about the frost on your neighbor's roof." Then he lay down on his bed and went to sleep. He discovered that life at home had never been so peaceful.

But one day he began to fear that these peaceful times were about to come to an end. On that cold winter day he had run smack into a group of thugs dragging a sobbing young woman into a dark alleyway. Song Shijie tried to restrain himself, reminding himself of his wife's warning; but it was no use and he jumped to the rescue. The ruffians, familiar with Master Song's temper, released the girl, and Master Song led her home, his heart full of misgivings. But to his great surprise, his wife was not angry, and even compelled him to take this "step-daughter" into the family. She also urged him to go to the *yamen* to file a lawsuit on behalf of the girl, whose name was Yang Suzhen. In this way, Song's wife repealed the prohibition on not minding other people's business on her own initiative.

Yang Suzhen's husband had been poisoned by her sister-in-law, the cunning Mrs. Tian, and Yang had been sold again to become someone's wife. When the cloth peddler Yang Chun heard the tragic story of the "wife" he had purchased with years of savings, he tore up the marriage deed, made her his adopted sister, and accompanied her to the *yamen* to lodge a complaint. It was on the way to the *yamen* that they were separated by the gang of ruffians.

The young woman had suffered many hardships in her life and wanted only to get her revenge. But she knew that depending alone on her own resources and the help of a good man like "brother" Yang Chun, she was bound to fail. But what could she do? All she had going for her was a pitiful story that evoked people's sympathy and the assistance of a powerless nobody. In the willow forest, a kindly fortune-teller wrote out a complaint on her behalf, and in the home of Song Shijie she received the sympathy of the old couple. Without hesitation she had knelt at their knees, finding security for the first time. From then on she was no longer fighting a battle singlehanded.

Song Shijie carefully studied the written complaint. Could a mere fortune-teller have the ability to write such a fine document? Even Song, with his years of experience filing complaints, was lost in admiration. He wanted to take his adopted daughter to the district *yamen* to voice her grievances, since his wife had asked him to hand in the complaint straightaway. But friends of his inveigled him into a tavern for a drink, and as a result he missed the morning session of the court. Just as the old man predicted, as soon as he got home he was bombarded with

Yang Suzhen's complaints. She spoke to her adopted mother, but the words were directed at him: "I'm not his real daughter.... If he hadn't gone drinking, the plaint would have been handed in straightaway." Song Shijie nodded his head and thought to himself: This new daughter of mine was a fine woman. Judging from what

she just said you could see that she was broadminded, astute and unafraid of officialdom. Nor was she cowed by the might of the *yamen* court.

The sound of drums beating before the *yamen* doors drove Gu Du out from the back hall, burning with fury. This circuit intendant had never met Song Shijie, but had heard all about him. He knew that Song had been dismissed from his post by one of his predecessors, but never imagined that the widow who lodged her complaint was living at his home. Thus he was seized with alarm when he realized that Song Shijie had come to lodge a complaint on her behalf. Meeting the old man face to face, he snarled: "Song Shijie, aren't you dead yet?"

As Song Shijie well knew this greeting had nothing to do with the case in hand, but was evoked by Song Shijie's past reputation, which made every official long for his early death. A person such as he could not possibly bode anything but evil for men of their profession.

"If an adopted daughter can't live in her adopted father's house, must she go and live in a convent? If a father doesn't care for his daughter, who is he going to care for?"

This silenced Gu Du completely and increased Yang Suzhen's awareness. As she helped the old man out of the *yamen,* she whispered in his ear: "Well said! Well said!"

Although Song Shijie's inn enjoyed a good location, business was poor. The inn stood outside the western gate of Xinyang Zhou on the main road into town. Occasionally traveling merchants too late to reach the city before the gates closed would put up there for the night, but they would always hurry off early next morning. This in fact suited the old couple very well, leaving them much leisure time. The old man enjoyed chatting with his customers, and after escorting them inside, filling a washing basin for them, lighting the candles and bringing them water to drink, he would sit down with them to discuss the local scenery, the market situation and the condition of the harvest, as well as news and gossip from near and far: he was interested in everything. Less talkative customers would simply eat, wash their feet, blow out the lamp and go to bed. Song Shijie would adjust his behavior according to his customers' different characters.

One evening, two guests dressed like officials and speaking in Shangcai County accents came huffing and puffing into the inn. They were carrying a small sealed wine vat which they placed on the table. They asked for a jug of wine to drink and closed the door of their room. Song Shijie was a wise old man and could tell at a glance that the two were in an awkward situation. The vat of wine was probably a congratulatory present. It was the custom to send a gift of wine when a baby was one month old — but such gifts were properly given in pairs. The vat of wine must have weighed only forty or fifty *jin* — light enough so that one person could carry two of them on a shoulder pole; but this vat was so heavy it required two men to carry it. Song Shijie came in with a jug of wine and placed it on the table. As he left, the man sitting on the left sighed, "Wine is a wonderful thing." The other replied, "Wine, wine, wine, day long drink your fill; The rich will go to Heaven, the poor will go to Hell." Although this was all Song Shijie heard, he was certain there was hidden meaning in their words. Years of experience in the *yamen* had taught him much and there was no form of skullduggery he hadn't encountered. Today's sighing and quoting of poetry were no ordinary occurrences.

Song Shijie guessed that their journey to Xinyang Zhou was related to the business of his adopted daughter. Later that evening, he stole into their room and from the breast pocket of one of the officials slumped in a drunken stupor on the bed, nimbly removed a letter in a large, red envelope. Criminal court clerks were usually adept at this kind of thing, and also well aware of the risk they were taking in doing so. It was all set out clearly in the *Statutes of the Great Ming Dynasty*. He sprinkled a little water on the envelope, unsealed it, took out the letter and read it, afterwards replacing everything exactly as it had been before. This was another of the essential arts a law clerk had to master. In less than half an hour, everything was crystal clear to him.

Two days later, Song Shijie once again accompanied Yang Suzhen to the district intendant's office to state her case. He knew what the outcome would be before they set out, but said nothing to his daughter. He knew that they would have to wear the cangue, that they would be forced under torture to confess to false charges, and that they would be found guilty and imprisoned. Nevertheless, he knew that his adopted daughter would be able to endure it, and that the case would have a great impact. Those involved were Gu Du, the local intendant; Liu Zhao, a district magistrate; and Tian Lun, a civil governor who had never taken office (he was the brother of Yang Suzhen's sister-in-law). The three of them had passed the highest imperial examinations in the same year, and were "three locusts tethered to the same string".

For Song Shijie, it was as if a large web with not one but three black spiders sitting in it were stretched out before him. He glanced at Yang Suzhen walking silently beside him. This young woman, hounded to the point where the only way out led straight into the spiders' web, knitted her lovely eyebrows in anger and trepidation. But her steps were resolute, honor allowing her no turning back. Outside the court room, Song Shijie waited for Yang Suzhen who, with the cangue around her neck, had already been taken into custody. He comforted her, "Off you go. But don't worry. It won't be long now. You can depend on your father."

Song Shijie rushed into the court and lodged an appeal against the decision. He knew well that this rash impulse would get him nowhere, yet he couldn't control himself. It was good to give vent to some bad feelings, since nothing disastrous could come of it.

But he had guessed wrongly, and suffered forty strokes of Gu Du's cane for "contempt of court and acting arrogantly with superiors".

After the beating, Song Shijie thanked Gu Du; this was the usual practice. Those seated above were always correct, those kneeling below were beaten, put in the stocks or even executed; but regardless of whether these punishment were right or wrong, the accused had to express their gratitude, since all punishments were carried out to "protect the people" by judges who "loved the people like their own children".

"Song Shijie, was the beating I gave you just?" Gu Du's smile revealed a set of pearly white teeth.

"Unjust!" Song Shijie gnashed his teeth in reply.

"Was I right to beat you?"

"You were wrong."

"Injustice is just and wrong is right," Gu Du concluded, adding, "From now on you should make yourself scarce around here. If you ever come here again, I'll have your life!"

"Who will be having whose life?" Song Shijie made his way out of the court. The night before he had carefully copied the secret letter written by Tian Lun to Gu Du onto the lining of the sleeve of his long gown. Now with the situation well under control, he sought revenge for his daughter and for himself.

Tian Lun, Gu Du and Liu Zhao went to the procurator's office to speak with Mao Peng, the head of the provincial court. Mao, the newly appointed civil governor of eight prefectures, had been personally appointed by the emperor, and bore the imperial sword which allowed him to order executions without imperial consent. Tian Lun was the civil governor of Jiangxi Province, but since the three-year period of mourning for his father's death was not over yet, he had not formally assumed office. Gu Du was the intendant of the Xinyang Circuit and Liu Zhao the district magistrate of Shangcai. The four held posts of different status, but had all passed the highest imperial examinations in the same year.

The provincial judge was already seated in court, with Tian and Gu in attendance. Liu Zhao's post was unimportant so he waited on the side, bustling about serving the others. Song Shijie had arrived very early and handed in his accusation. As he waited his turn to be called, he saw Tian Lun and Gu Du being escorted into the court and saw Liu Zhao waiting by the door. Song Shijie had read the *Records of the Imperial Examinations*—no one who worked in a *yamen* was unfamiliar with it. Everyone knew who had graduated with whom, who came from which county, and each successful candidate's predecessor, examination supervisor and patron.... *Yamen* employees had to be thoroughly familiar with this myriad of relationships, which was all set out very clearly. That the three men accused by Song Shijie — Tian, Gu and Liu — had passed the examination together suggested that they would assist each other in covering up their evil doings. But was Mao Peng also involved in their intrigues? Who could tell?

Song Shijie waited anxiously. When Liu Zhao was asked to enter the court, his anxiety deepened. Was this tied up with his case? Were the strings really being drawn tighter and tighter? Only when Liu Zhao, stripped of his hat and robe, left the court mopping the perspiration from his brow could he relax a little.

Gu Du came out of the court and went up to Song Shijie. Pointing at him, he said: "This time when you see the judge, say what you ought to say and don't talk nonsense!" Song Shijie looked at him and laughed:

"I'll say what I ought to say. But as for what I shouldn't say, well, maybe I'll say a few words." Song Shijie felt reassured: he began to see which way the wind was blowing.

Quite unexpectedly, the provincial court judge came straight to the point and asked Song Shijie to describe every detail of the case. Tian Lun and Gu Du gave the old man warning looks and mouthed soundless threats, which Song Shijie pretended not to notice. He said everything he ought to as well as everything he "ought not to say", finally producing the jacket with the letter copied onto the lining, which even Gu Du knew nothing about.

In the end, Mao Peng made allowances for the two men who had graduated with him, protecting their dignity by not allowing the plaintiff to see how he dealt with them. Song Shijie was ordered to leave the court temporarily while the sentence was handed down, and Gu Du quietly followed him out.

"Song Shijie, come back here! That's a formidable jacket you have."

"My Lord, you have a formidable cane!"

"Huh! When I get back to the *yamen* I'll have your life!"

"Ha! What makes you think you're going back there?"

Song Shijie was right: neither Gu Du nor Tian Lun returned to their former offices.

Song Shijie embraced Yang Suzhen with tears pouring down his cheeks. He felt as if he were in a dream. Why should an old man like him have to be exiled? Was Yang Suzhen really his own flesh and blood? As if these questions had occurred to him for the first time, he was momentarily unable to come up with any answers.

But Song had even greater misgivings. The case had been won without any effort on his part. A single accusation had downed three officials. But this was a "miracle", and he knew from experience that such a miracle was unprecedented. Could such a court as this exist anywhere in the world? Song Shijie confided his fears to his daughter, indicating the "honest official" sitting upright in the judge's seat. Yang Suzhen brushed away her tears, and went to express her gratitude to that "honest official". When she returned she told Song Shijie that this "honest official" had a strong resemblance to the fortune-teller in the willow forest who had written the original plaint for her. But this was no mere resemblance; it *was* him.

Song Shijie asked: "Are you sure? Haha — then I won't be exiled!"

For an official to write an accusation on behalf of one of the masses was illegal — this was clearly stated in the *Statutes of the Great Ming Dynasty,* and both Song Shijie and Mao Peng knew it well. One had defended an innocent person against an injustice, and the other had broken the law out of the goodness of his heart. Even an "honest official" was capable of getting around the rules and understood the virtue of "flexibility". Song Shijie was not exiled after all.

The Case of a Man's Head

During the Jia Jing period (1522-1566) of the Ming dynasty, the emperor devoted all of his time to practicing Taoism and neglected attending to state affairs, and so for more than 20 years real state power lay in the hands of the prime minister Yan Song (1480-1567).

Yan Song and his son were treacherous officials who curried favor with the emperor because of their ability to write elegant essays. Once having attained positions of power, they persecuted many upright fellow officials and embezzled astonishing quantities of funds and property from the people and the imperial treasury.

Mo Huaigu had a treasured family heirloom, a jade cup called "A Handful of Snow". On behalf of Yan Song's son, Mo's friend Tang Qin tried to extort the jade cup from him. However, when Mo tried to pawn off a counterfeit cup on him, Tang quickly saw through the deception and Mo then fled with the real jade cup. Later, he was arrested and handed over to be executed to the renowned general Qi Jiguang (1528-1587), the garrison commander stationed at the Great Wall.

— Ed. —

Lu Bing, chief of the emperor's Brocade Guards, sat in his official chair in the court room, rapping on the table with a folded fan. It was a gloomy day and the room was

205

cold and cheerless, and the chief felt an irrepressible heat and dryness in his heart. Since he had taken charge of criminal affairs, with authority over the Six Boards of State, this was the first time he had had to handle such a singular and annoying case.

His task was to try a man's head: to judge whether it belonged to a convicted official, Mo Huaigu, who had recently been executed. Mo Huaigu had refused to give up a valuable heirloom, a jade cup called "A Handful of Snow", to the house of Yan, whose master was no less a personage than Prime Minister Yan Song, and had escaped the latter's wrath by relinquishing his post and fleeing. He had been captured, together with his mistress Xueyan, and executed summarily under the eyes of an official dispatched from the house of Yan. All this had been perfectly clear and the case should have been closed, but a number of unexpected complications had arisen.

What annoyed him the most was the man now sitting at one side of the judge's table. Sent here by the house of Yan to take part in a joint hearing, Tang Qin was only a minor official, but he had strong backing. Ostensibly he was a second to Lu Bing; in fact, however, he was the boss, and the authenticity of the head rested upon his word, not Lu Bing's. The great chief of the Brocade Guards was only a puppet here, which of course was not to his liking.

Disputes as to whether the head was real or fake arose as soon as the hearing began.

Lu Bing had questioned several witnesses, among them the official sent to make the arrest and Mo Huaigu's mistress Xueyan, and their statements corroborated. From the moment of Mo's arrest to his execution and the placing of the head in a wooden box, nothing questionable had been detected. Nevertheless, the single word

"false" casually uttered by Tang Qin, sitting at one side with his eyes half closed, was enough to reverse the verdict. Tang sat there swaying his torso and along with it the plumes on his official cap. This little man possessed a diabolic power that not even the chief of the emperor's secret service could counter, though it incensed the latter to no end.

The "Brocade Guards" was an organization controlled by and responsible to the emperor himself. Though the functions and powers of this organization had already been vested in the various governmental departments, it stood above the Six Boards of State, and had greater latitude in the use of its powers: it was the real government with real power to rule. Besides, it carried out many tasks of great secrecy for the emperor. For instance, the "Red Riders" under its command could arrest, try, sentence and execute people at will. But Prime Minister Yan also had his own "private army", whose omnipresent agents conducted searches and arrests that grossly encroached upon the authority of the Brocade Guards. And now Tang Qin had received orders from Lord Yan to sit at a joint hearing with Chief Lu Bing. It was as good as riding on his neck.

A malicious thought entered Lu Bing's mind.

"Your Excellency Tang, you keep insisting that this head is a fake. Can you point out the distinguishing features on Mo Huaigu's head?".

Lu Bing knew all about Tang Qin's background. He knew that it was on Mo Huaigu's recommendation that Tang Qin became a retainer in the house of Yan, and yet had the conscience to divulge to the Prime Minister the secret of his former master's jade cup — a betrayal so contemptible that even Lu Bing would have shuddered and turned bright red. But this meant very little to him right now; after all, he had seen much more and much worse. What he wanted to know but could not guess at present was why Tang Qin should cling so obstinately to his claim? What great enmity was there between him and Mo Huaigu? A curiosity peculiar to his profession overwhelmed Lu Bing.

"His Lordship Mo had two noble features on his head: jaws of affluence and bones of nobility at the back of his skull," answered Tang Qin, giving the grounds for his verdict in a categorical manner. At this, Lu Bing, the man in charge of criminal affairs, could not but feel admiration for the man. Still, he was unclear about the real intent of Tang Qin's seriousness. As he meditated, Tang Qin, knowing that his explanation could not stand on its own, proceeded to offer more details in a frank and somewhat passionate manner:

"In my less fortunate days of yore, I sold calligraphy and paintings at Qiantang to earn my living. One day, Lord Mo, returning from visiting friends, passed by my shed and saw my calligraphy in regular, cursive, official and seal scripts and my paintings. Being a scholar with compassion for talented men in need, he engaged me as a retainer in his household. Later, when summoned to the capital as an official, he took me along with him. On the way, we slept together at inns, washed from the same basin, hung our clothes on the same rack, and ate from the same table; thus I observed everything plainly and clearly."

Lu Bing's doubts were not dispelled, but Tang Qin's words had certainly moved him. That he had noticed Mo Huaigu's affluent jaws and noble skull could not by itself determine whether or not the head belonged to Mo, for this was merely a verbal report. But Tang Qin displayed deep feelings when recalling those past events: when he spoke about his good fortune, he began gesticulating with both hands and feet; and when he expressed gratitude to someone who had recognized his talents, his eyes were tender and passionate. He regretted that there were any real doubts about the head. Had it unquestionably belonged to Mo Huaigu, he probably would have clasped it to his breast and wept out loud.

Lu Bing sighed. "I despise Mo Huaigu for his poor judgment; and I mock him for recommending somebody that turns out to be an iron-clad witness against him!" These caustic remarks of his pleased him, and he hoped that they would soften Tang Qin's rigid attitude. He wanted to use this opportunity to settle the case. Tang Qin, however, stood up to take his leave; he was going back to the house of Yan to report to the Prime Minister that the hearing had been inconclusive. Lu Bing was on fire; this scoundrel was too crafty and too stubborn, and had a thick skin insensitive to shame; there was no way to get to the bottom of things and uncover the mystery. For when you advance, he retreats; when you stop, he stops too; and when you return to your place, he starts advancing.

In a rage, Lu Bing declared that he and the Prime Minister were officials in the same court. They both served the emperor, so why should he fear the Prime Minister's power? His language was violent and his voice compelling, but Tang saw through it at once: he was merely putting on an act. "Is Lord Yan a wolf or a tiger?" Lu Bing asked.

"If he's not a wolf or a tiger, he's at least as awesome!" Tang Qin answered.

"The emperor stands above and the good earth below. For officials like you and me, what is most important?"

"A good conscience."

"And if they had no conscience?"

"If they had no conscience . . . let the Heavenly Dog eat them up!" said Tang Qin without batting an eye; but he gnashed his teeth and shouted, "Eat them up!" as if the Heavenly Dog were there.

Lu Bing had nothing more to say. It was clear that he was no match for this rascal. Stealing a glance at Tang Qin he noticed him wearing that perplexing smile that expressed neither joy nor anger; it was more like a mask that he wore on his face all day, which caused only boredom and uneasiness in people who were unable to guess what lay behind it.

But even the most carefully laid plans have flaws, and every cloud has its silver lightning. Lu Bing reflected: Old Tang's expression was not immutable; only the changes were so small and fleeting that they often passed unnoticed. For example, on the two occasions when Xueyan was being questioned, he was unusually attentive, which was not his normal behavior. He listened with his mouth half open, completely absorbed; his eyes followed every move, every twitch and smile of the girl so closely that he did not even heed the questions put by Lu Bing. From this it appeared that the identity of the head and the pleasure or displeasure of the Prime Minister all hinged upon the fate of this girl.

Lu Bing now held the key that would resolve all the problems. But as he did not want to resign himself to total defeat at the hands of that rogue and lackey Tang Qin, he could not make up his mind.

Even the chief of the ruthless Brocade Guards could not totally disregard public opinion. If in closing the case he should openly award Mo Huaigu's mistress to Tang Qin, the risk he faced would be far greater than that

involved in killing a few convicted officials or bandits. He had already been given assurance by Tang Qin that he did not have to press the case any further; this came after he had granted Tang an opportunity to try Xueyan behind closed doors, which would allow him to go ahead and close the case without worrying about the authenticity of the head. But this was an act of expediency, involving a secret deal that the public did not know about. Pronouncing the verdict in an open court was a different matter, and even a butcher like Lu Bing was not insensitive to the power of feudal ethics.

Xueyan appeared to be far more clever than Lu Bing. During her short "trial behind closed doors" she told Tang Qin that their relationship began two years ago when they were on their way to the capital. One day while stepping into a boat, she slipped and nearly fell into the water, but Tang saved her in the nick of time. Thereafter, His Lordship had always held a foremost place in her heart.

Xueyan's courage and determination were indeed greater than Lu Bing's. Back in the court, when Lu Bing continued to shillyshally, unwilling to put his name to the document, it was one of Xueyan's remarks that prodded him into action. "How muddleheaded His Lordship is!" With his eyes half closed, he wrote out the verdict and awarded Xueyan to Tang Qin. Since everything was predestined, what else could he do? Moreover, wasn't Xueyan willing to go along with this?

The next day, Lu Bing sat dumbly in his study in a wretched mood, waiting for the public censure that was sure to come. He sat there until midnight, when the people he had dispatched to Lord Tang's wedding ceremony returned. They brought back a shocking report: Lord

Tang, intoxicated with drink, had been murdered in the bridal chamber. His new bride, too, was dead. The news brought Lu Bing to his senses. In an instant he understood everything and this made him feel very small. "For shame!" he muttered to himself; and then, reassuming a serious look, called out, "Saddle the horses! We're off to the bridal chamber for an autopsy"

Lian Huan Tao

Dou Erdun was a Robin Hood-like outlaw who was active in Hebei Province during the early Qing dynasty (1644-1911). The story of the struggle between Dou Erdun and the father-and-son duo of Huang Santai and Huang Tianba, a man in the service of Qing Emperor Kangxi, was first popularized by itinerant storytellers and later included in the three novels "The Cases of Lord Peng", "The Cases of Lord Shi" and "The Cases of Lord Yu". The tales contained in these three novels are all based on true events and the lives of real people, which have been elaborated into fascinating stories.

The main characters in this play are the "wusheng" (warrior) Huang Tianba and the "hualian" (painted face character) Dou Erdun. During the 20s and 30s of this century, the striking makeup and startling acrobatics of Yang Xiaolou in the role of Huang Tianba and the bold gestures and resonant singing of Hao Shouchen in the role of Dou Erdun made quite a sensation.

— Ed. —

Dou Erdun the stockade chief sat in his golden chair before the Hall of Heroes, his eyes closed in tranquil repose. Not a muscle on his face moved, however hard the sun was shining upon it. This was something that had not happened for a long, long time.

In a tournament 30 years before, Dou had been knocked off his horse by Huang Santai, a professional armed escort, who, however, had resorted to trickery to accomplish his aim. As the disgrace was too much for the ambitious young warrior, he had fled to this mountain hideout called Lian Huan Tao where he concealed his name and identity. Several decades had passed in the twinkling of an eye, but his thirst for vengeance never left him and his soul had not a moment's rest. All these years there was no news of Huang's whereabouts, so he could not seek out his rival for a return bout. His anguish was like a worm gnawing at his entrails.

Liang Jiugong, the emperor's favorite eunuch, was on a hunting trip in the country. For miles around the story spread that he had brought with him, or rather "escorted" to the hunting grounds, an imperial steed awarded him by the emperor. The bridle and saddle of the horse were of bright yellow gold. The animal ate over ten measures of black beans a day, plus grain and hay, a diet richer than a poor man's. It could travel "1,000 *li* by day and 800 at night" and was waited upon by several dozen soldiers who groomed, watered and watched over it day and night.... This story was stretched more and more until the stockade chief felt that something had to be done. To him, the rumors were both absurd and nauseating, so he thought up a trick that would give the emperor and his pompous eunuch a bit of annoyance. One night, under cover of darkness, he went down the mountain, stole into the imperial camp and, after killing a night watchman, released the steed and rode it back to his mountain stockade. Just before leaving the camp, it struck him that this was a good opportunity to get his revenge, so he scribbled a note on a wall linking the theft

of the horse to his enemy Huang Santai. Since he had not been able to trace the whereabouts of his enemy, he might as well let the emperor and his eunuch concern themselves with it. His little trick had come off so smoothly that he was pleased, and though he was now relaxing with his eyes closed, his stout body swayed instinctively with pride.

Even the report that one of his lieutenants, who had gone down the mountain on an errand, had been captured failed to move him. His only order was for the others to find out how the land lay and effect a rescue if possible. What finally made him leap from his chair was the name card handed to him by this lieutenant who had been released. The card, so it seems, was from that formidable armed escort who had unseated him years before, here now to pay a courtesy call on the mountain stockade. The card read: "Huang of Shaoxing Prefecture, Zhejiang ".

"Isn't this the enemy I have been looking for for years?" he asked himself, and then cried out loud: "How old is this man?"

"About thirty." His spirits dampened quickly on hearing this. "Show him in," he said in a lazy voice, then carelessly tossed the card aside. Still, at the suggestion of his lieutenant, he ordered his men to "line up and greet" the visitor.

His young visitor was Huang Tianba — the son of Huang Santai — a public official as well as a professional armed escort. He had come to the stockade after making a thorough study and analysis of the situation. The words on the wall left by Dou Erdun had linked his life and family fortunes with the fate of the imperial steed. If this horse were not found, it would mean the ruin of the Huang family. He concluded that even if the horse were not in this stockade, he should be able to trace its whereabouts here.

Huang Tianba was a shrewd man. He went up the mountain alone not because he was bold but because the life of the horse was at stake. It would have been an easy thing to have the imperial troops surround the mountain stockade, but the horse would be endangered if they did

219

so. He had to place the safety of the animal above his own life, and relied on his own cunning and ability to deal with emergencies as they arose. His hopes were pinned on the ideals of chivalry which had benefited both he and his father in the past. He understood the weakness of such men and how to make use of it. That was why he had maintained so many ties with them and even now was only presenting himself in a "semi-official" capacity.

When they met, the stockade chief tried to induce Huang Tianba to join his band, at which the latter concluded that the old chief was just as naive as he had been in his younger days. The hardships of life had not eaten away very much of his forthrightness. Huang declined modestly but did not refuse altogether; he responded by a lavish display of enthusiasm and good-will, declaring that his sole purpose in coming was to offer the chief the clue to a very good deal.

"And what may the prize be?" asked the chief, appearing somewhat swayed.

"A most valuable steed," answered Huang, lowering his voice to a solemn and confidential whisper.

"Ah, but we've got plenty of good horses here, there's nothing wonderful about that," remarked the chief, now appearing to lose interest.

Winking and moving his chair to Dou Erdun's side, Huang began whispering to him about how the horse was a supernatural animal, peerless throughout the world. He was trying to provoke the chief. If the imperial steed was indeed in the stockade, the chief would not be able to hold out against such boasting and sooner or later would divulge something. He had guessed right; his devious plan had succeeded.

For a time the chief listened patiently to the rambling talk, but when he was told that the great family which owned the horse employed no less than 300 members of its household, plus 200 trainers, to look after the animal, his patience ran out. However impressive this was, he did not believe it could stand comparison with the pomp of the imperial camp that had guarded the steed now in his possession! Several times he thought of interrupting Huang's nonsense; finally he seized him by the wrist.

"Are you serious about making friends with me, or just pretending?"

Huang gazed into the chief's flashing eyes and knew he was about to get what he wanted.

Receiving a worthless "assurance" from his adversary, Dou Erdun made haste to tell the whole story of how he had sneaked into the imperial camp at night and stole the valuable steed. Huang was overjoyed to have discovered at last the whereabouts of the steed, but he hoped to be able to see it with his own eyes to make sure it was still alive and well. So to cover up his joy and surprise, he shook his head skeptically and stared blankly at the narrator. The latter, seeing his dejected looks, burst out laughing.

"I knew you wouldn't believe all that." So saying, he made a gesture with his hand and his subordinates standing below the hall hurried away. In a short time, the imperial steed was brought before them. The grooms pulled at the light yellow reins with all their might but could not keep the powerful beast under control; it kept moving its front hooves as if in great agitation.

It was now the stockade chief's turn to be surprised. The gallant young armed escort appeared to be bewitched. He stood at one side of the horse's head as if rooted to the spot, silent and motionless for some time. Then suddenly, with the speed of long practice, he let down the cuffs of his long sleeves, bent one knee in salute, and then dropped down on both knees.

These strange acts surprised everybody including the chief, who did not know what to make of it. "A country bumpkin!" he said at last, thinking he had formed the right judgment of the man, but he was quite wrong.

The armed escort prostrated himself before the horse for a long time, with his head buried in his sleeves. He was thinking how he could get the chief to tell him the real purpose of the note he had scribbled in the imperial camp. What was the subtle relationship between this stockade chief and the Huang family of armed escorts in Shaoxing?

Rising quickly to his feet, he stood straight before the chief and blurted out: "It's a good horse, but unfortunately quite useless now."

"Why is that?" asked the chief, and he went on to explain that he stole the horse not to ride it but to use it to avenge himself on his enemy and his family. At this point he suddenly remembered the name card and began eyeing the man before him suspiciously.

"This enemy of mine comes from the same place as you. . . . Not only that, he has the same family name. . . . He's that armed escort Huang Santai!"

"His Lordship Santai!" said Huang Tianba, folding his hands together in salute.

"That old nobody!" the chief cursed at the top of his voice.

"But Chief, you'll never get your revenge."

"Why?"

"Because His Lordship Santai's returned to the Western Heaven."

The news was indeed a shock to Dou Erdun. This was the day he had been waiting for for several decades, during which he had not only veiled his name and identity but also endured humiliation and disgrace. Now all his hopes were shattered. The chief uttered a long sigh, venting the hatred he had nourished for years and the enmity that would never fade. He gnashed his teeth; his eyes were on fire: "Yes, but the man's family is still there!"

A moment later, Dou Erdun became aware that the young armed escort was none other than the son of his enemy, Huang Santai. Not only was he continuing his father's profession as an armed escort, but had also inherited his treacherous nature. His scheme to visit the stockade was obvious to all. Dou Erdun found this intolerable, and seized Huang Tianba by the arm. He shouted:

"Huang Tianba, you villain, your father is dead! I will now avenge myself on you!"

How surprised all those in the hall were when Huang Tianba burst into laughter. This laughter was so hearty that it seemed it could only come from the mouth of an outspoken but sophisticated and worldly person, though a slight trembling revealed the fear which lay in his heart of hearts. He retorted:

"I am unarmed and surrounded by your people. Come forward."

Faced with Huang Tianba's disdainful but hypocritical countenance, the stockade chief retreated. He decided to give up his plan of dealing with him right away and took up Huang Tienba's challenge of a martial arts contest on equal footing. He even went so far as to call on the relevant officials to confess his crime in the event he was defeated. In this way, he proceeded step by step from this first retreat to total failure.

Not long afterwards, Dou Erdun and his sworn brothers began to fade from the arena of history. Lian Huan Tao became deserted, or was perhaps leveled to the ground, and to this day the precise location of the site remains unknown.

Sister Thirteen

During the first half of the 19th century, the Manchu nobleman Wen Kang wrote a novel in the Beijing dialect entitled "The Gallant Maids", which achieved wide popularity at the time. This novel recounts the story of a love affair between He Yufeng, an errant swordswoman, and the scholar An Ji. Ever since this story of how the heroine carried on a tender romance with the hero and battled despots to protect the weak and downtrodden was first performed on stage, it has been warmly received by Chinese audiences and has become a standard item in the repertoire of traditional Chinese operas.

The opera's title, "Sister Thirteen", originates in the fact that He Yufeng lived under this assumed name when she stalked the man who slew her father, in order to avenge his death. The second character in her name, "Yu" (玉), can be read as a combination of the two characters 十 (ten) and 三 (three), which when taken together mean "thirteen" in Chinese.

The story below is an episode from the full-length opera.

— Ed. —

He Yufeng gave her donkey a few kicks and it trotted briskly up the slope. Shading her eyes with her hands, she scanned the dense forest before her and adjusted the bow slung across her back and the handy little dagger at her waist. She looked around for some time until her panting had subsided, but still nobody emerged from the forest. She was beginning to lose patience.

This was the road leading south to Shandong from the capital. Early in the morning when she had just started out she had chanced upon a group of three — two roguish-looking donkey drivers escorting a youthful scholar. She had merely glanced at them and hurried past, for her black mount with its white belly traveled much faster than their caravan. After a while, however, for some inexplicable reason, she began to feel uneasy, and turning around circled behind the three and came upon them in the forest again. While resting here, she overheard their conversation and learned that the scholar was on his way to Huaiyang. The two donkey drivers were most servile towards the young master, but they never removed their eyes from the heavy baggage on the donkey's back. She sensed at once that something was wrong. As she had heard them say that they were going to deliver an important letter to Red Willow Village and would pass the night at the Yuelai Inn further down the road, she decided to go on ahead and wait for them at the inn. Up to now, however, they had not left the forest and her mind was beginning to waver; it seemed odd that she should be so concerned about the safety of a stranger she had met only by chance. What business was it of hers? Still, she could not put it out of her mind. For she was quite sure something unfortunate would befall that young man that very night or the next day, and if she did not help, would she not be considered an accomplice?

Dismounting in front of the Yuelai Inn, He Yufeng surveyed the whole place. It was a sizable inn. Two large willows stood before the door, with trunks so thick that a full-grown person could barely embrace them. Three or four draft animals were tied to the trees and a large unharnessed wagon stood close to the wall. Inside the entrance, one could see a large courtyard with guest rooms lining the four sides. Thd kitchen and stables were in the back yard. The inn assistants rushed in and out, carrying food and water, for the sun was setting and it was time for the evening meal. In the corners of the yard flower beds and rockeries were scattered about.

The manager of the inn was watering the flowers when he saw He Yufeng enter and rose to greet her with a broad smile.

"You want a room for the night?" he asked, eyeing her from head to toe. The jet black donkey she was leading told him part of the story.

"My donkey's thirsty. Water it, please," she said, giving him the reins. "As for me, I'll just rest here in the yard. Get me a pot of tea." So saying, she pulled over a bench and sat down beside a flower bed. She glanced at the guest rooms, nearly all of which were occupied. Sure enough, in a room on the inner side of the courtyard was the young man she had met on the road earlier in the day. She knew, too, that he was looking at her from behind the curtain, and broke out in a broad smile.

He Yufeng removed her hood and gently fanned herself with it, at the same time smoothing the wisps of hair at her temples. She felt a bit uneasy, for it was the first time that a young man had ever looked at her so closely, and from a place of concealment. She laughed at herself: Why had she followed him for no apparent reason and then placed herself here to be spied upon? She could not account for this and began to feel a wee bit embarrassed. The next minute she heard a clang and knew that the door behind the curtain had closed. This vexed her as she could not imagine what was in the young man's mind. She might just as well move her seat forward and sit right in front of that room. She was sure that he was peeping through the slit in the door; if he wanted to, let him look at her as much as he liked.

The young man peeping out from behind the closed door saw a girl with a countenance both solemn and angry. His uneasiness increased; and the bow on her back, the dagger at her side, her fierce eyebrows and stern features all proved that his fears were not unfounded. Though he had not seen much of the world and only knew from books that there were women knight-errants, he could tell at once that the person sitting before his door was one of them.

The door opened again quietly and the young man raised the curtain and slipped out. He tiptoed past the girl and walked over to the flower beds. Was he there to enjoy the flowers? He ran his eyes over the rocks, rolled up his sleeves, and stooped down and tried to move one of the larger ones.

He Yufeng could not imagine what he was up to. He called over the manager and four or five assistants, but none of them could move the rock either. By this time, her patience ran out and she came over for a look.

"You want to move this rock?" she asked, examining the rock. "Where do you want to move it to?"

He was so astounded that he could not answer her. It was only when she asked a second time that he pointed in the direction of his room and said, "Over there, to my room."

He Yufeng now understood why the young man needed the rock — to place against the inside of his door so that no intruder could get in. And very likely the intruder he feared was none other than herself, a girl in such strange attire. Though she had long been accustomed to people looking at her with suspicion, this young man's actions were unprecedented. She was both humored and annoyed, and decided to play a trick on him. Sizing up the rock, she bent down quietly, grabbed hold of the jutting edges and raised it from the ground. Then, with a meaningful glance at the young man, she turned and walked towards his room.

There were now only the two of them, and the rock, in the room. All the onlookers had dispersed. She sat down in a chair beside the window and smiled mischievously at the young man, who stood dumbly by the door.

Questioning a wealthy but unsophisticated young man was more difficult than interrogating a rogue or even a river bandit, but it was also more interesting. In the face of her questioning, he stammered and dodged, trying to use what little cunning he had to cover up facts that he had already divulged. He wore a long face and backed down repeatedly in attempts to patch up the loopholes in his "fairy tale". His wretched looks and incoherent speech were as laughable and pitiable as they were vexatious, but she pressed on relentlessly. Her voice was generally harsh, but occasionally seemed sympathetic and consolatory. She could not understand why this was so — why her heart should soften at times. The young man also noticed these subtle changes in her feelings. It was a long ordeal indeed, from the moment she had placed the rock on the floor and sat down, when he had fallen upon his knees to implore the "great queen" for forgiveness, to when he was finally convinced that she was a true "heroine", a chivalrous woman, and began addressing her in this way.

He spoke the Beijing dialect, but insisted that he was from Baoding; he was a young gentleman whose worldly experience had not passed beyond the walls of his study, but he identified himself as an office assistant on his way to his post in Henan, forgetting that he was on the road to Shandong; he had with him 3,000 taels of silver, but he admitted to only 900 and nobody believed him. The girl pointed out all these lies to him and rebuked him:

"You fool! Your life's in danger and you act cunning with me!"

In the beginning it was only out of curiosity that He Yufeng tried to draw out the young man's life story. But when she learnt that his father had been imprisoned on a false charge and that he was taking silver to Huaiyang to ransom him, she sighed in sympathy, for her own family fortunes were much the same. She, too, was a victim of political intrigues. Her father had been persecuted to death and she and her mother had had to change their names to escape from their enemies. She assumed the odd title "Sister Thirteen" and thereafter led the wandering life of a knight-errant. She who would have passed her days peacefully and happily in a boudoir, and he who would have passed his in a study, were brought together in this wayside inn by a twist of fate. Their haphazard entry into each other's lives gave rise to a strange attachment and led to a series of episodes equally strange.

He Yufeng felt sympathy for this helpless young man that she herself could not account for, and believed that it was her duty to help him. First, she had to help him escape being murdered by the two donkey drivers; then she had to escort him to Huaiyang and collect enough money for him to ransom his father. The young man was now so moved that he again fell on his knees. This made her feel very awkward, for she disliked seeing others humbling themselves before her. She was ready to do what she could to help him, but did not want to be rewarded in any way.

She was about to bend down and help him to his feet when suddenly she became conscious of her femininity and drew back. Though nobody had seen her, she felt her cheeks turning red. Quietly she took the bow from her back and thrust the tip towards the young man.

"Take hold of that and get up," she said in a soothing voice. Her voice sounded strange even to herself, as if suddenly she had become another person.

京剧故事集

黄　裳　著

＊

新世界出版社出版（北京）

外文印刷厂印刷

中国国际图书贸易总公司发行

（中国国际书店）

北京399信箱

1985年　第一版

编号：（英）10223—156

00700

10 - E - 1966 P